Publish and be damned
www.pabd.com

Life, Love and Assimilation

Kia Abdullah

Publish and be damned
www.pabd.com

First published in Canada 2006 by Kia Abdullah

Designed in Toronto, Canada, by Adlibbed Limited.
www.adlibbed.com

Printed and bound in the USA or the UK by Lightningsource.

ISBN: 1-897312-00-8

*Thanks to Zeeshan - my rock,
Shiri for being my first and most
positive reader and Rabika, Siedah, Rita
and Rashanara for being who you are.*

Chapter 1. The Ending

The family sat in dark silence. Not everyone of course for even in death, they were divided. The sisters sat on the sofa in a stunned silence. Rayya wiped again at her tear-stained face. The children's laughter drifted down the stairs. Most of them were too young to understand the situation. The older ones were torn between their playful younger siblings and the sombre moods of the adults, so they sat in the kitchen trying to hear what was being said, which of course was nothing.

The father was the most composed. Outliving any of his daughters was such an absurd idea that it had not sunk in. The sisters had never experienced the death of a loved one so they had no idea what the routine was. The funeral was being arranged but of course, they would not be allowed to attend. It had happened so quickly. The fire had spread out of control in a matter of minutes. Kieran had been at the heart of the explosion; the only fatality. And now she was gone and all that had been said was, "Does anyone want some tea?" That was the curse of their culture; nobody said what they felt, nobody talked to each other. Everything was stored away and allowed to fester.

So here they were: the five remaining sisters, the father and the mother; everybody thinking but not talking. Rayya, being the most emotional, had spent the day crying continuously. Jasmine had rallied everyone around and kept herself so busy that she did not have time to hurt. Shelly was tired; she had driven down from Manchester and felt exhausted by all the drama. Neha had made endless cups of tea and kept thinking about Kieran's dying moments; she must have felt so scared, so hopeless, so utterly trapped. Kieran had died in exactly the same way she had lived, and that was the thought that hurt the most. Sania just felt guilty about having continuously rebelled against Kieran, and now she was gone - burnt alive; vaporised; thin air.

The phone rang incessantly and finally roused her from her deep sleep. Neha tossed in her bed and checked the time. 1pm. *God! How long have I slept?* she thought. She answered the phone and offered a groggy "Hello?"

"Hi, Neha?"

"Yeah?"

"It's me, Zahid."

Neha sat up in bed.

"I've been trying to get hold of Kieran for a few weeks now but I haven't been able to reach her. Does she have a new number?"

Yesterday's events hit Neha like a speeding train. "Um, she's dead," she said flatly.

"Neha?" he questioned, "It's *Zahid*. I wanted to talk to Kieran."

"She's dead, Zahid. She died yesterday. There was a fire and she got caught in an explosion. Everyone was at the New Year's party but she went down to get the camera and something blew up. Everyone got out but her." She said the words for what seemed like the hundredth time since yesterday. By now she could say them without her voice cracking.

"Neha, that's not funny. Seriously, please tell her I want to speak to her."

"You're not listening to me. She's dead. She's gone."

"Are you being serious? You don't even seem upset," he said.

"She's dead. That's not a joke. Now you can believe me or not. I have to go." She hung up and tossed the phone onto the bed.

"What the hell?" Zahid said to himself. He dialled Neha's number again but received no answer. "What the hell!" He paced his room and tried Neha's number again: nothing. "What a sick joke. What's she on?" He tried Kieran's mobile a few times but it was switched off. He knew Kieran had told him time and time again to leave her alone but she would not go to lengths such as these. Not even Kieran would go this far.

He sat on his bed and tried to shake the feeling that had begun to creep over him. "No," he said to himself firmly. He then switched on the television and settled into his bed. After a few minutes of channel-surfing he switched it off again. He grabbed his phone and this time dialled Kieran's home number, a number she had told him never to dial. After a few rings, a female voice answered the phone.

"Hello, Asalam Alaikum."

"Hello, this is Mr. James Baker at Barclays Bank. I was hoping to speak to a Miss Kieran Ali," said Zahid.

"One minute please."

Zahid almost shouted in relief. The woman on the phone was fetching

Kieran. He had not believed what Neha had told him but he had had to check. *Kieran's gonna kill me for calling her house,* he thought. *I'll just pretend I am the bank guy.* She was probably going to recognise his voice anyway but it seemed like the safer option.

"Hello?" The phone was finally picked up again.

"Hello, is this Ms. Kieran Ali?" he asked, trying to disguise his voice.

"Who's this?"

"Hi, this is Mr. James Baker. I am calling from Barclays Bank about your statements."

"I'm afraid Kieran is not here right now."

Zahid tried to figure out who he was talking to. "Um, well, when will she be back?" He tried to keep the confusion out of his voice.

"May I ask what exactly this is about?"

"It's, uh, regarding the frequency of her statements. She recently called about receiving her statements more regularly and I was just chasing that up. I can't authorise the transaction until I speak to her. May I ask who I'm talking to?" he asked, thinking quickly.

"I'm her sister, Jasmine Ali. I'm not quite sure about your procedures in this kind of event Mr. Baker but Kieran was," a pause, "she was involved in an accident a few days ago, um, a fatal accident. It came as a shock to us all, as you can imagine. We are all in a state of disarray so if you could please… " Jasmine's voice drifted off.

Zahid dropped the phone. His head felt heavy and he shook it to clear the fog that had begun to form there. He couldn't think. He felt faint and sick all at the same time. He felt himself crumple down onto the floor where he sat still, not daring to think, not daring to feel, not daring to breathe.

When Zahid finally came out of his state of shock, night had fallen. He glanced at the clock and blinked a few times. He knew that tears would not come. He had been through it all before. The ever-present lump in his throat would not dissolve. The tears would not be wept. The bitterness would not fade. He placed his head in his hands and tried to abate the rising anger inside him. He refused to believe that someone so alive could be dead; that someone so precious could be stolen; that someone so scarred could be wounded further. She had always had faith; faith that

God would give her good things to balance out all the afflictions she had endured but now she was gone - killed when she still had so much left to see, so much left to do, so much left to say…

Chapter 2. My Childhood

One of my earliest childhood memories is when I was four years old and on my first visit to Bangladesh. I was sitting on the porch dressed in a ragged pair of shorts and a ripped T-shirt. My Aunt had spent the morning trying to get me into a dress but being the tomboy that I was, I flat out refused, opting instead for the "street rat" look that I was now sporting. I remember shielding myself from the scorching sunshine that beat down on my neck and hurt my eyes as I looked out onto miles and miles of yellow fields. The air smelled of burnt hay as it always did in Bangladesh.

Suddenly, I spotted a woman wearing a pink sari walking in the far distance. I stood up and yelled with joy. I ran barefoot through the rice fields towards the figure in the distance. It was my mother coming back from the market. She had left early in the morning whilst I was half asleep. I vaguely remembered the pink sari when I woke up and demanded to know where she was. I had spent the next two hours crying and moaning because she had left me alone in this strange country full of cows and hay and people who stared. I had then gone out onto the patio to await her return. As I watched the pink sari in the distance, I was so happy and relieved that she had returned.

That sounds pretty normal, right? Well, that's funny because that occasion is the one time I felt what could be described as love towards my mother. As an adult, I can't even imagine missing her. The thought actually disgusts me and I am embarrassed to admit what I felt then. But we will come to that in good time because, as any good psychiatrist will tell you: all our problems, insecurities, fears and fuck-ups stem from our parents.

Growing up, I always felt a sense of disquiet; a sense that at any time the floor would be pulled out from under me and that I would land flat on my face or maybe disappear into a hole altogether. It's funny how we worry about so many things when we are children, things that don't really matter in the long run.

When I was ten years old, I broke my nose whilst playing a game of 'high-jump' at school. Basically, we strung all these elastic bands together, two people held it on either end at varying heights and the player jumped over it. A friend and I jumped at the same time and her head banged against my nose. Even though it hurt like hell, I did not tell a teacher because I knew that my parents would be called and that I would get into trouble for playing the game. I sat through school all morning with a broken nose until at lunch time, a teacher noticed that my eyes were swollen and bruised. My parents were called and I was sent home. I was so worried that I would be told off if I told them the truth that I lied and said that a girl had run into me in the playground. Nonetheless, my mother shouted at me for being so clumsy and warned me to watch where I was going in future. My father wrapped me in my oversized coat and took me to the hospital. I could see tears of worry in his eyes. Even at that young age, I remember thinking that my dad was too old for worry. His fifty-four years showed through his greying hair, wizened skin and thin frame. He was always the one who took care of us, who told my mother to back off when she got too much. I just wish he had told her to back off more often.

They say that appearances can be deceptive which in my experience is absolutely true. My mother looked like the quintessential loving matriarch of an Asian family. She was round and plump and soft-looking. She was always swaddled in a billowing sari and wore her hair curled up in a tight glossy bun. Despite being in her forties, her Asian skin was only faintly wrinkled. She would chew on betel nut between meals and periodically spit into the sink the earthy red juice that reddened her teeth. She would stand in the garden gossiping with our next-door neighbour for hours, talking in hushed tones and laughing out loud. Inside her plump exterior, however, lay a cold, hard, woman. She bore eight children; six daughters and two sons. She lavished affection and forgiveness on her sons and reserved all her scorn and anger for her daughters.

The reason behind this is probably very simple. In a lot of Asian cultures, it is seen as good fortune to bear a son whereas a daughter equals a big burden, especially when it comes to marriage. A girl has to be guarded more closely; her honour more fragile than that of a boy's. A girl is weak and will leave her parents once she is married. In a way, she never really belongs to her parents at all but to her future husband and his family. She is never really an 'asset'. A boy, on the other hand, grows up to be strong and hard. A boy can work and feed his parents long into adulthood. A son is the biggest asset one can have: this is the attitude of many Asian people and certainly the attitude my mother had chosen to adopt.

After her first two daughters and two sons, she wanted one more son. She became pregnant and gave birth to a daughter, which filled her with disappointment. She became pregnant again, hoping for a son. But she gave birth to me, which filled her with anger. She became pregnant again and yes, again gave birth to a daughter. This filled her with bitterness. She became pregnant for the eighth time in total and what happened? She gave birth to a daughter. This was the final straw and drove her to become a bitter, twisted and hateful person. All because she had four daughters in a row when all she wanted was a son. So who is to blame? Well, the daughters of course! There were six girls in the family, which is a nightmare for any set of Asian parents. There was an eighteen-year gap between the eldest, Rayya, and the youngest, Sania.

I remember a neighbour of ours, a white man called Bob, once commented that my parents must be so proud to have such beautiful daughters. My mother simply clucked her disapproval and turned away. The eldest two of my sisters, Rayya and Jasmine, were treated relatively well since they were not born into the 'cursed' era but the rest of us were always made to feel like a great burden.

As my mother went about the housework, she would ask out loud for God to kill her, to bring death to her, for what had she done to deserve this life? What abhorrent crime did she commit in order to be punished with us? When I was younger, I used to think, *If she hates her life so much, why not just kill herself?* The answer of course being that in our religion, suicide is one of the greatest sins and a sure-fire way to secure a place for yourself in the everlasting fires of hell. Of course, she wasn't a religious person. If so, then why did she hate us so much? Why did she favour her sons so much for, in Islam, is favouritism amongst your children not also a sin? But as I shall explain, my mother's scorn was one of the only constants in our lives of instability.

I woke up before dawn with a mixture of sadness and excitement. August 9 1992: my eldest sister's wedding day. The colourful decorations had all been put up, unabashedly Asian in their brightness and gaiety. Strips of red, green, yellow and orange crepe paper spiralled the black iron gates that lined our front yard. A big sign written in Bengali and adorned with gold tinsel welcomed guests to the house. It all seemed magical to me. I walked down the stairs of the silent house, soon to be filled with people rushing around trying to get everything and everyone ready. I walked into the kitchen and glanced at the counter laden with sweets. I resisted the temptation to slip a *ladoo* or *jilabi* out of one of the boxes to sweeten my mouth. Everything seemed so untouched and almost perfect even its state of disarray that I did not dare disturb anything. At dawn, the first signs of a sunny day appeared and the house began to stir. One by one my family awoke and the preparations began.

The house filled with relatives and friends. Aunties and uncles whom I barely knew squeezed my chin and commented on how much I had grown and how I was so much quieter than when I was younger. As the bride's sister, I felt so important as I walked around. I had on my favourite dress patterned in green floral with my hair in a neat oily plait.

I wheedled my way into Rayya's room. She and her friends had said that no kids were allowed in the room as they prepared her but I felt that I was an exception. I watched intently as they applied a thick layer of makeup on her face, accentuating her eyes with heavy kohl. They brushed her hair until it was silky and smooth and then tied it high upon her head. They patterned her feet with mehndi and then eventually weighed her down with all her wedding gold. She was impeccable in her red and gold sari and her sad eyes made her the perfect bride.

And like the typical bride, she was late to the wedding hall, which was shimmering in red and gold. She sat on the stage like a regal princess: demure, sweet and silent. The rest of us ate with gusto. Delicious tandoori chicken with fresh salad; *Pilau* rice and plain rice served with hot meat dishes; vegetable curry seasoned heavily with turmeric and chilli. And when at last everyone was sated, it was time for the great farewell. Slowly they walked my sister out of the hall, supporting her small frame. As she approached the long white stretch limousine, she started to weep. I was sad but not sad enough to cry for some reason. I watched my mother hug my sister with tears in her eyes and even though I was only ten years old, I felt a sense of falseness in that simple action. Maybe it was genuine emotion but I simply smirked and took a step back.

With all the drama over, we set off home. I yawned as we walked into the empty house. My father grumbled quietly about the mess the children had made. He was awfully house-proud which is strange, I suppose, for someone who didn't really own a house. We lived in a huge three storey house which belonged to the council. Our rent was paid by housing benefit as my father was unemployed... Well, on paper anyway. Back then, I never questioned the fact that the house didn't *really* belong to us; it was just the way things worked.

I used to share a room with Rayya and I thought that the only good thing about her going away was that now I got to share with Shelly who was the sister I was closest to. As I walked into our new room on the top floor, I jumped onto the bed in an exhausted heap. I looked forward to sharing a room and long conversations deep into the night; to sharing secrets, dreams, hopes, fears and laughter. Little did we know that our time in that room would bring nothing but terror and sadness.

"Get out of the room," he snarled. I stood there, saying nothing. "NOW!" He advanced on us. Shelly had already scampered off the bed and out of the room but I just glowered. *"Tafa kayter?"* He threatened to slap me.

"Room taki baroyza," my mother called up the stairs telling me to get out of my room. I got up and stormed out angrily. She wanted me to get out so my brother could search our belongings for the sixty pounds that had gone missing from my father's room. I was confused. I knew that neither Shelly nor I had taken the money so why were we being accused? As if I would have the audacity to steal sixty pounds! That amount of money was so inaccessible to me that I could not even conceive of possessing it, let alone hatching a plan to steal it and spend it. It may as well be a million pounds for all I was concerned.

As this thought trailed off in my mind, the door to our room slammed shut. He was inside pawing through our things with complete freedom even though we were innocent. I stood burning from a sense of injustice. It still makes me so angry to think that at that point, my parents had also known we were innocent. I was too young to realise that my brother was a thief and stole everything he could in order to fuel his drug habit. My parents knew this but denied it and even if they had accepted it, they would not dream of confronting him about it. So there I was, banished from my room, filled with an intense sense of injustice. I was too young to understand; too young to articulate what I was feeling. It was a mixture of fear, anger and frustration. Moments later the door was ripped open, my brother's face black with anger.

"Where is it!?" he screamed at my sister and me. "I know you took it. Where is it!?"

Shelly cowered under his raised fist. I stood still. He slapped her head then grabbed her shoulders.

"I didn't take it!" she screamed but his face was now a mask of rage, devoid of any human emotion.

He shook her, screaming, "Give it to me! Where is it!?" He continued to shout as she fell back. He kneeled down and grabbed her hair, pulling her up by it. He punched her in the chest. She screamed in pain as he hit her again and again. Eventually, with his energy spent, he allowed her to drop to the floor. I stood like a coward filled with a mixture of anger at what he had done and relief that I was not the one on the receiving end. I also remember the tinge of shame that followed the feeling of relief.

"I'll find it," he said and walked off.

My mother came upstairs and looked at us. "If you took the money, just give it back," she said. "We won't say anything."

As I grew older, this type of beating occurred often. Back then, I did not understand why he beat us so much when he knew we were innocent. I now know it was all just a great big show to prove that it wasn't him that took the money; that he was angry at the thieves who *had* taken it and that he was on my father's side. I realised that my parents knew he regularly stole and lied but he was their precious son: how could they possibly accuse him of such crimes?

I was lucky, for I had been given a defiant nature by Allah and I was never scared of my brother. I always stood my ground and did not worry about getting hurt. This is probably one of the reasons I was not hit very often; because I was not worth the fuss. I used to go crazy if he laid a hand on me. I would scream, shout and threaten to call the police. Shelly, on the other hand, was an easy target. Constant berating from my mother had ebbed away her self-esteem over the years until there was nothing but a shell; a punch bag for all the things that went wrong in my mother's, and brother's lives. I now wish that I had gone crazy all the times he had hit her too. Even though she was four years older, I was the stronger one and I could have protected her more. I developed a thick skin. I ignored my mother's constant criticisms but Shelly absorbed it all, taking in every last word and tried her best not to believe any of it. Maybe it was because she was the first of four consecutive daughters that she was treated so badly. Maybe my mother was just evil to the core but every day, Shelly, as well as the rest of my sisters, was reminded about the burden we had placed on my mother just by being born as women. In our culture, men were so valued and so respected that they could be forgiven for anything. *Anything*.

Sania's small frame shook as she walked down the street to our house. Her eyes flowed with tears and she was wracked with sobs she couldn't expel because she found it so hard to breath. She stumbled into the house in a flurry of tears.

"What's the matter?" asked Jasmine. She shouted up the stairs for me to come downstairs.

I flew down the stairs at the urgency of her tone. I looked at Sania sobbing against the door. "What happened? What's the matter?" I asked Jasmine.

"I sent her to number twenty-eight to return the video film we borrowed and she came back like this," she replied. "Sania, what happened? Did someone say something? Did they start on you or tease you about something?"

Sania shook her head and simply cried harder.

Jasmine held her by the shoulders, kneeled beside her eight-year-old frame and tried to calm her. After a few minutes, Sania's body stopped shaking and she started to breath through her sobs. "What happened?" Jasmine asked again.

"I went to their house," she started, her words barely intelligible through her sobs. "And their dad opened the door. I gave him the video and he told me to come in. He took me to the living room."

Jasmine and I exchanged a quick look. "And then?" urged Jasmine gently.

"He sat on the sofa and sat me on his knee. There was no-one else there… and then… ” She stopped as fresh tears streamed down her face.

"Sania, what happened?" I asked firmly.

"Then he pointed to here." She gestured to the area between her legs. "And he asked 'What's under there?'"

I recoiled in horror, never before knowing such anger and disgust. Sania's body started shaking again.

Jasmine grabbed her. "What happened next? San, you have to tell me. What did he do?" she asked.

Sania shook her head. "Then I got scared and he let me go."

"He let you go?" asked Jasmine.

Sania nodded.

"Did he do anything else? Sania, you have to tell us the truth. Did he get on top of you?"

Sania shook her head.

Jasmine looked at me and said, "Call the police." I didn't question her. At this point, I was crying too and dialled the number in a blur. I informed the police of what had happened and was told that a pair of officers was coming to our house.

At that moment, my mother walked in and laid eyes on the scene. We both explained what had happened. She looked at us blankly and then looked at Sania coldly. "Are you lying?" she asked.

I felt as if I'd been slapped.

"She's not lying!" screamed Jasmine. "We've called the police and they said - " She was cut short by mother's thunderous shout.

"You did WHAT!?"

"We called the police," I said.

"You stupid idiots," said my mother. "You stupid bloody idiots! God knows what people will say when this gets out! Do you know how much shame this will bring on us? If the police come here, people will want to know what it's about. Do you know what people will say? *Oh, Allah! amare kizati furutain disore?"* She threw up her hands in despair. In all my years of enduring my mother's verbal abuse, I don't think I had ever felt such hatred for her and as much disbelief at her actions as I did then. I was in utter shock that even though this dirty old man had done something so monstrous to my eight-year-old sister, all my mother could think about was what other people would say.

I looked at my mother in disbelief. "Do you *realise* what just happened? It's not Sania's fault! Why should *we* be ashamed?" I asked.

She looked at me viciously. "You're an idiot. You won't understand. This will bring shame on us. Call the police back and say it was a mistake."

"No," I replied.

"Call them now!" she yelled. Sania stood in the corner with Jasmine. "Don't you understand? They will take her to court and make her explain what happened and everyone will know. Do you realise how shameful that is? Call them back now!"

"We can't let him get away with this!" I yelled back.

"You're a child. You do not understand. We can't let this get out."

"No!" I screamed back and ran upstairs in fury.

Eventually, she made Jasmine call back and tell the police that it had all been a misunderstanding but they insisted on coming by anyway. I refused to tell them that everything was ok. The police specifically wanted to speak to the person who called them: me. By that time, Kamal had come home. He told me to go downstairs and speak to the police, to tell them it was a joke. I told him I wouldn't. They spun a story about how I was scared I was going to get told off because I made a story up and the police left it at that. I suspect they weren't convinced but what else could they do?

Jasmine and I told my other sisters what had happened but how could we tell our father? Yes, it *was* a shameful and embarrassing thing; something that a daughter could never discuss with a father. My mother did not tell my father what happened but after I saw him shake the man's hand one day, I went berserk. I screamed at my mother and told her to tell my father or I would. I was not there when she did but from that day forth, my father never spoke to that man and never went to their house again. The whole event was swept under the carpet and forgotten, as are so many things in our culture. A man commits such a great crime against a young girl and everyone forgets it because it is *shameful* and *embarrassing*. The man lived on happily with his wife and children whilst we only hoped that Sania would forget about what happened too, and particularly forget how my mother made her feel like it was her fault that it happened.

Yes, my mother may have shouted and screamed at her children; she may have hit them and abused them verbally and mentally but up until that moment, I expected her to protect her children from external sources of harm when she needed to. I expected maternal instinct to kick in and I knew in that single moment that it would not. My mother had not protected her child when need really called for it, and that was her biggest failing both as a mother and as a person.

As time went on, things became worse. We lived in constant fear that Kamal would have an outburst and decide to take it out on one of us. We felt trapped and vulnerable. Eventually, it just got too much so we did the only thing we could do - planned to run away. Shelly was working at 'Burger King' and had saved enough for a deposit on a room. A 'room' being just that: it had a bed, a kitchenette and a chest of drawers; she shared a communal toilet and bathroom. Every morning, Shelly snuck out our belongings bit by bit. She would take them to the room then leave for university. We were so excited about leaving home. We hid suitcases under our beds and talked long into the night about what we would do with our new-found freedom. Looking back, I am shocked at how naïve we were. I was fifteen and Shelly was eighteen. It's weird how you think you know the whole world at that age. Yes, we had been through tough times and were a bit wiser perhaps than our peers but I don't know why we thought we were tough enough to strike out on our own. It was desperation more than anything. At the time, it was something we had to do. We planned excitedly and budgeted our living costs to what we thought was accurate.

As the day of reckoning arrived, we could barely contain our excitement. We woke up at the crack of dawn and crept downstairs. Immediately, we realised that something was wrong. The front door was locked from inside. No one ever locked it and yet on that day, it was locked. We searched for the keys frantically. The time had come and we didn't want to spend one more second in the house. Shelly hid her small bag in the kitchen and we continued to search as silently as possible. Suddenly, we heard Jasmine's voice behind us.

"We know," she said simply. We both turned in shock. "We know everything. We know where you hide your suitcases. We know when you planned to leave. Do you think we're stupid?" she asked angrily.

Before we could ask her not to, she was up the stairs waking my parents. I remember feeling scared for my life. I was frozen in fear. I wanted so much to get away from my family; coming so close and having it snatched away like this was heartbreaking.

I have never been shouted at as much as I was that day. They sat us both in the living room and one by one interrogated us and shouted at us and insulted us. It struck me how they were so confused as to why we wanted to leave. They kept asking, "Why?" But how could we explain if they did not know already? We felt trapped, we were allowed no freedom whatsoever, and were subjected to endless criticism every day. We could not explain so we both stayed silent.

More than anyone else's, I remember Jasmine's words. She turned to Shelly and said, "You can forget about university. You can forget about going out. You can forget about your life. You just destroyed everything you had."

Jasmine, our big sister, had caught us and though she was one of us, she had always sided with my parents. I always felt a sense of bitterness from her. I think it was because she was prohibited from going to university whereas Shelly had been allowed to. By the time Shelly was of university age, it had become a little more acceptable to allow one's daughters to go to university. Despite this, I still could not fathom why Jasmine should feel any type of jealousy toward Shelly who was treated like a slave, but there it was. Jasmine's tone was victorious with a sweet smugness that sickened me. I knew that what she said was true though. I was young and mentally strong but Shelly would literally be locked up in the house everyday and, as Jasmine had so succinctly put it, her life *would* be over.

You can forget about university. You can forget about going out. You can forget about your life. You just destroyed everything you had. Those were the words that pushed Shelly over the edge. She called the police because she just could not handle it anymore. When the police arrived, my mother was furious. I felt like I was trapped in a nightmare. Shelly told the police that she wanted to leave and that my parents would not let her. I could not go with her because I was only fifteen and under my parents' guidance. I wasn't worried though because I knew I could handle it. It was Shelly I was worried about. Dad came into Shelly's room whilst the police were watching her gather her belongings. He started to cry and beg her not to go. He kept saying over and over, "Don't go. Please don't go. What have we done?"

As much as I love and respect my father, asking her that question made me angry, for what they had done could never be verbalised. How could she answer that question and truly show how deeply she had been scarred? She, also in tears, left with the police to her new room and to what she thought would be her new life.

Months passed and, surprisingly, things at home got a bit better. My mother and father had several screaming matches and my father finally told my mother things she needed to be told. He said it was her fault that Shelly had left and that she needed to stop treating us the way she did. I knew that inside she boiled with anger but from that day forth her complaints were daily instead of hourly. She still demanded rather than requested but that I could live with.

Shelly called me regularly. During one conversation, she told me that my father had been turning up at her workplace every day, begging her to come back. I told her to stay strong but I could tell she was wavering. How on earth could she work when my dad was in the corner of Burger King every day begging to talk to her? I could imagine the embarrassment and shame she must have felt.

Shelly could not afford to leave her job because she was just about keeping her head above water. My mother still refused to accept the blame for what had happened and constantly went on about how Shelly must have run off with a boy and how it was the only explanation. Of course, I knew that this was not true.

Things went on as usual until one morning I woke up to find two black bin liners at the foot of my bed. I felt a cold fear course through my body. I turned to Shelly's bed, expecting her to be there. I thought that perhaps they were her belongings and that somehow they had forced her back home. I breathed a sigh of relief to find the bed next to me empty. I crawled to the foot of the bed and tentatively opened one of the bags.

I gasped as I saw Shelly's clothes and books stuffed in there haphazardly. *What the hell is going on?* I quietly stepped out of my bedroom, looking for more clues as to what had happened. As I was just about to place my foot on the top stair, I heard a cough from the room that Javed, my eldest brother, used to occupy. No one had lived there since he'd moved out. I crept towards the door praying that I would not find Shelly in there. I opened the door quietly and felt my heart sink as I spotted her lying there in the bed.

I crept over to her and shook her awake gently. "Shelly, what's going on?" I asked.

She rubbed her eyes and sat up. She had a defeated look in her eyes. "I had to come back."

"What happened?" I asked desperately. I had wanted her to leave this place so much. It meant no more beatings for her, no more locking up her belongings, no more suspicions or accusations.

"They followed me home. I didn't know. They knocked on my door last night at 11pm. Someone else let them into the building and they practically broke my door down with their banging."

"What did you do?"

"I opened it. I had to or other people would have started to come out."

"Who was there?"

"Dad and Kamal and *Dula-bhai.*"

My father had taken my bastard brother and Rayya's husband with him. I had known nothing of this plot. "What did you do?" I repeated.

"I didn't know what to do." Her eyes filled with tears. "They packed my stuff and told me I was coming home. I couldn't say no. I was so scared."

I felt so bad for her. I felt angry and sad and defeated. "What are we going to do now?" I asked.

"Nothing. There's nothing we can do."

Shelly stayed in her room the whole day. She could not bear to face the family. She had paid her rent for the remainder of the month and was completely broke. My parents allowed her to keep her job. They tried to keep a balance between being strict and not pushing her too hard.

No one ever said anything about the episode and even though it had bought much pain and anguish to the family, my mother realised that she was not invincible and that her actions did have consequences. From then on, Kamal's beatings of Shelly stopped and my mother became a little more tolerable, so the whole disastrous event did have a positive result.

Weeks passed and things were calmer. Weeks blurred into months and then into years. Jasmine was married off and we all grew older. Jasmine's husband had been born and raised in Bangladesh and then had moved to New York for seven years. After marrying him, Jasmine moved to New York for three months and we went to visit her. It was one of the best times in our lives as we were allowed two weeks away from the family. When we came back, our spirits immediately blackened. My brother's drug habit had only deepened. The smell of weed emanating from his room had been replaced by something darker and more sinister. We knew he was taking class A drugs and was becoming increasingly desperate for his next fix. I lost many possessions to his thieving hands. It taught me not to covet material things because I knew that nothing of that sort was safe in our house. I had always yearned for a mini-disc player, for example, and two weeks after I finally got one, it went missing.

I was often amazed at how he managed to find money I had hidden in places I thought no one would think to look. I taped it behind posters, put it in my underwear draw, and hid it in the packets that held my sanitary towels but it always went missing. We all had locks on our doors which were locked when we went out but not when we were watching television or eating in the kitchen and that's when he would sneak in like a snake, sniffing through our belongings.

My father transferred money for people from the UK to Bangladesh. He often kept money at home and had it go missing regularly, and I am talking thousands here. Kamal snuck in and struck in an instant, in the a blink of an eye. I suppose you almost have to admire his speed and expertise. There were regular arguments with my parents over money issues. They finally decided to confront him about his habit but of course they only did so half-heartedly. I think at that point everyone knew it would be ridiculous if he continued to blame his sisters for the disappearance of the money so he either denied it or ignored their accusations. Not that he was ever *accused*, simply *asked* if he had happened to come across a bundle of cash hidden away in the depths of my father's closet and if it had somehow ended up in his pocket.

Living with him and witnessing everything he did and got away with built up hate inside me. I truly hated him for everything he did, even during those years after the bad beatings had ceased. Well, ceased until one day I came home from work and found my mother sitting in the living room with a stony face.

"What's the matter?" I asked.

"Talk quietly," she said.

"Why? What's wrong?"

"He hit Neha," she replied simply.

"Kamal?"

"Yes."

"Why?" I asked calmly.

"Because he found the benefit book in her room."

My parents were both unemployed and lived off Income Support. My mother's Child Benefit book, which was used to withdraw money from the Post Office, had gone missing. Kamal had accused us of taking it. He had gone into Neha's room and searched for it. He had said that he found it under her bed and had hit her. At that moment, I assumed it was once punch or one slap and that made me angry enough.

"What? You *know* she didn't take it! And you let him hit her? You didn't do anything?" I asked.

"Keep your voice down. He is upstairs."

"So what? I don't care if he's upstairs!" I screamed. "You always hide away from him. You always let him do whatever he wants. He gets away with everything!"

She didn't say anything for a moment. "Be quiet and go upstairs," she dismissed me finally. I was fuming with anger and ran up the stairs in fury. I went to Neha's room and saw her sitting on her bed, shoulders drooping and her head down. Sania was sitting on the floor.

"Neha? Are you ok?" I asked.

She looked up with tears in her eyes and shook her head. The side of her head was swollen.

"What the hell?" I went closer to examine her head. It was puffy, swollen and bruised. "What happened?" I asked.

Neha didn't say anything so I turned to Sania. "Sania, what happened?"

"He beat her up coz of the benefit book," she replied.

"Tell me what happened, exactly."

"He started to get angry coz Mum asked him if he had seen her benefit book. He said that one of us took it. He told us to get out of our room and he searched through our stuff. About three minutes later, he came out with the benefit book in his hand. He said that he found it under Neha's bed. He grabbed her without even saying anything and started to hit her." Sania paused.

"Go on." I felt the anger rise.

"He grabbed her by the neck and slammed her to the floor. He then hit her head against the bin again and again." Sania started to cry. "I was there and I couldn't do anything. I was frozen. I didn't even call Mum and Dad. I stood there coz I was so scared. He kept slamming her against the bin again and again."

"Where were Mum and Dad?" I asked.

"Downstairs. They came after about five minutes coz they heard Neha screaming. Dad stopped him but he was going to hit Dad. Then he just went into his room and we went downstairs."

I was so angry, I wanted to kill him. I wanted to open his door and kick the shit out of him, the way he had done to my little sister. I shook with fury and the knowledge that there really was nothing I could do. I went downstairs and screamed at my mother.

"Why didn't you do something? Do you know what he did to her? Don't you care?"

"He wasn't thinking straight," she replied.

"Thinking straight? The bastard never thinks straight! He's going to kill one of us one of these days and you're not going to say a word because 'Oh, he wasn't thinking straight'!" My mother said nothing. I wanted to scream in frustration. I wanted to shake her and get her to wake up. I wanted to ask her why there were no boundaries when it came to my brothers but so many when it came to my sisters and I. I wanted to scream and shout and yell at her but of course, I said nothing. I simply walked out and went to my room.

I wanted to cry. I could not believe it. I was so tired and all I had wanted was a shower and food and this is what I came home to. I went to college five days a week studying A-Levels and then worked all weekend. Seven days a week I worked, studied, exhausted myself. He sat at home all day, stole from my parents, inhaled away his Jobseeker's Allowance and treated our home like a hotel; leaving dishes for the maids to carry away and wash, leaving clothes to be washed and ironed. And he should not have hit Neha. He had hit us all in the past but he simply should not have beaten her up like that. Neha was sixteen, a year younger than me, and had had a hearing defect since birth. Her hearing impairment had stunted her learning ability and therefore she always needed help when dealing with the external world. I knew that she would grow to be independent in the future but at that moment in time, Sania's ten-year-old English was better than Neha's and so Neha had no confidence when talking to others on her own. There was no way in the world she would autonomously decide to steal the benefit book, go to the post office and cash the giro on her own. No way in the world. I knew that, he knew that and my parents knew that but still this was allowed to happen.

Neha drew into a shell after that day. She jumped like a cat anytime someone touched her and she would not go near Kamal. One day, when we were about to eat rice, he was in the kitchen. I took her food to her in the living room. When I came back to wash her plate, he was at the sink. I stood next to him waiting for him to finish with a defiant stance.

"You think you're so brave, don't you?" he said without turning to look at me. "When I kick the shit out of *you*, then you will learn," he said and walked out.

I wasn't scared of him though. I never was. Sania, being the youngest, used to ask me why I didn't call the police to have him arrested. I knew that it would not hold. It would be a waste of time. The police could not do anything. Neha would break under my mother's pressure and I simply did not have the energy. Everything else he did was petty theft and 'mild' physical abuse which I knew would not hold any water in court. If they let murderers and rapists go after a few years in jail, what would a slap or a punch or a kick mean? It scarred us all physically and psychologically but legally, it meant shit.

And so the years rolled on. Things got better and things got worse. I made plans as did we all. I aimed for university. I would have loved to move out but in Bengali culture, that just wasn't the done thing. An Asian girl living alone is a slur on the family's dignity and respectability and so I knew there was no hope until after I finished university. I was still doing my A-Levels and I just had to wait. The only thing we could do was survive.

Chapter 3. My Corruption

They say you make your friends for life at university. They say university changes who you are. Despite my problematic home life, school life had always been good. My four best friends had always been there for me throughout school and college and I knew that they always would be. You can't choose your family but thankfully you can choose your friends and what Allah did not give me through my family, I was given through my friends. I obtained three A grades at A-level, which was a feat, considering that I attended a school in Tower Hamlets, the third poorest borough in Europe. I believe that another reason I did well academically was in order to balance out everything I went through at home. Overall, I was doing okay. Life had made me strong. I was ambitious, determined and focused. I did not know how university was going to change me but I knew that I would always be strong.

I stepped into what they call the 'Queen's Building' and asked where Room 430 was. The Receptionist told me I was in the wrong building and that I needed to take various rights and lefts, climb some stairs, navigate a mixture of corridors and "hey presto." I couldn't ask her to repeat all of that so I left with my sub-standard navigational skills and continued my quest. I scratched my arm which itched underneath the acrylic material of my deep red zip-up top. I had teamed it with a pair of old jeans, done my long black hair up in a ponytail and hoped I would fade into the background.

This was it: the beginning of uni life. I was excited and scared and nervous and happy and worried and all the things you should be when you're thrown into the deep end. I had chosen to study Computer Science at Queen Mary, University of London. It wasn't a bad university. It wasn't one of the best either but it was a fifteen-minute walk from my house, which my parents were happy about. What kind of mischief could I get up to when I was practically on my doorstep?

I suppose they thought that suddenly unleashing me into a mixed gender environment would turn me into a man-hungry nymphomaniac. I had attended an all-girls school and stayed on at its Sixth Form college, which was also all-girls. I had some interaction with boys at work but I could not say I had any male friends. Uni was going to be interesting. I knew that I wouldn't mess around with boys though. I didn't have the time or energy for them. Throughout school, tons of girls had raced through boyfriends like there was no tomorrow. I always felt pity for them because I felt that there was nothing else in their lives. They did not have any ambition; they were happy to study their GCSEs and then live off the dole for the rest of their lives, just like Kamal. I had big dreams, big hopes. I had started from the dirt of East London but I wanted to see the world, I wanted to be somebody. I wasn't going to be content being someone's wife or daughter or mother. And university was the first big step towards my dreams. Boys just weren't a part of it.

"What's your name?" he yelled back at me from the front of the lecture hall.

"Kieran!" I shouted back.

"What!?"

"Kieran!" I shouted again.

He nodded and turned back.

The cacophony quietened as students found their places and readied themselves for the second week of lectures.

"Who's that?" asked Zain.

"Some guy I met in the ITL. I don't know his name," I replied and turned to the lecturer at the front of the room. The first week of university had been good. At first I couldn't believe that I had come to a place where I knew no one at all to study a subject I knew nothing about. Only five students from a body of two hundred in my year at Sixth Form College had gone to university so there was no way I could have come to university with a friend. Luckily, Zain, who worked at the same place I did, was studying the same course. I worked at a Market Research Centre as a Telephone Interviewer and knew him in passing. Seeing each other at university made us stick together - glad that we had found a companion.

The rest of the week went by in a blur. Orienting ourselves and getting into the swing of things took time. I met lots of new people and became slightly freaked out that I understood nothing in lectures but the promise I felt in my heart did not fade. I knew that I was going to enjoy uni life.

"He is cute!" I said to Ashley, eyeballing the teaching assistant.

"For God's sake Kieran, you have the worst taste in the world," she replied in exasperation.

"He *is!*" I insisted. "Look at his eyes."

Ashley just sighed and shook her head at the worksheet. We were sitting in a long room doing a 'Logic Lab', which basically meant working through a worksheet in small groups. My table consisted of me, Ashley, Zain, Aisha and Zahid. The worksheet was a jumble of symbols and letters and I didn't pay too much attention to it, devoting it instead to Jules Bean, our teaching assistant for Logic. He was every inch the English gentleman but had the whole scruffy genius thing going on as well. He had wavy dark brown hair and the most impossible green eyes I had ever seen.

"You fancy him?" asked Zahid whilst examining Jules.

"I just think he's cute," I repeated with a shrug. Zahid had sat at our table uninvited but we didn't mind. The groups were split into different times and his usual group of friends had been put into the next slot. He was the guy who had asked for my name in the lecture hall during the second week of university. He was funny and made us all laugh and therefore was okay by all of us.

"Jules Bean? He looks like a woman and has a name like a cartoon character," commented Zahid just as Jules approached our table.

Aisha stifled a giggle.

"How's it going?" he asked us casually.

"Yeah, okay," replied Zain, hoping that he would not ask us any questions.

"What question have you come up to?" he asked, glancing in my direction. I stared back blankly as I had not even done question one.

Ashley came to my rescue. "We're up to number six," she said, shoving her sheet at him. He took it and looked it over approvingly.

"Excellent, carry on," he said and walked off.

"Those eyes! Those eyes!" I whispered in a Frankenstein "It's alive! It's alive!" manner. They laughed and Zahid shook his head. He was probably thinking that we were a bunch of weirdos which I guess we were.

Zain was an Asian East End boy hoping to do well academically whilst retaining his street cred. I don't think that was something he needed to worry about. He got teased by his friends from 'outside' but I knew that they respected him hugely for getting to university. He was tall and good-looking with thick dark hair and dark brown eyes. He had a penchant for designer clothes that his bank account couldn't really handle but which made sure he always looked effortlessly cool.

Ashley was what she liked to call a 'Chinese Giant.' She was 5'6" which was not particularly tall but she always went on about how most Chinese men were shorter than her hence making her a 'giant.' She had beautiful shoulder-length hair and flawless skin which I always grumbled about. She was clever but a tad lazy. If she was any more laid-back she'd fall off her chair but it was the thing I liked most about her. She didn't try to be cool or clever and, apart from an occasional grumble about being a size 14, she didn't care about her looks, unlike most of the girls at university who were completely absorbed by their appearance.

Aisha was a rare breed. She was a short and petite Bengali girl like me. In fact, if you looked at us from behind, you would be forgiven for thinking we were twins. However, our physical appearance was the only thing we shared. Her attitude towards life was so different from mine. I saw life as something to fight through, she saw it as something to embrace, along with all the people in it. She truly believed in the best in everyone. She was innocent to the brink of naivety but I knew she possessed a deeper level of wisdom that most people didn't understand.

Other members of our motley crew included James, a private-school educated Muslim boy who drank alcohol, went clubbing and was the funniest person I'd ever met. Then there was Adnan, the boffin who never quite made it, and Farah, the shy one. We had somehow banded together in the first few weeks of university and though we didn't all see eye-to-eye, we got on well and had similar attitudes towards study. We worked hard at getting everyone in the group up to speed with work but were just as happy to laze around at the Balcony Café all day missing a day of lectures.

As the lab approached its end, I wondered if teaching assistants were permitted to date students. Not that I would, of course, because as I've said, I didn't have time for boys.

Weeks passed and my crush on Jules became a bit of a joke in my circle of friends. One day in a lab, I turned to Ashley. "I'm going to ask him out," I said.

"But he's engaged," she replied, only half listening as she thought I was joking.

"I know but I may as well."

"What do you mean 'you may as well'?"

"Well, I know he's gonna say no so there's no fear of rejection."

"But if you know he's gonna reject you, why ask? Fool," she stated and went on with her work.

I pulled down my black slash-neck top so that it exposed a little more of my shoulders and then got up and walked over to Jules. Ashley watched me but didn't say anything. She couldn't hear what I was saying to him.

"Jules."

He turned to look at me. "Yes?" *Those Eyes!*

"Do you have a girlfriend?" I asked.

"Uh, yes," he replied uncertainly.

"That's too bad because I was going to ask you out," I said simply.

He looked at me and coughed. "Uh, she's my fiancée actually," he said, telling me what I already knew.

"Really? Congratulations."

"Thank you," he replied.

"How long for?"

"Since August."

"Wow. No chance of an affair then?" I watched the blush spread on his cheeks.

He laughed. "No, that's sweet though," he said in his middle-class Cambridge educated accent. I smiled and walked away. So that was out of my system. It wasn't the usual type of thing that I would do but he was there and I was there and what the hell? I went back and sat down.

"What did you say?" asked Ashley eyeing me with suspicion.

"I asked him out and he said he's engaged," I replied simply.

Ashley studied my face, trying to work out if I was serious. She laughed at me and went back to her work. I returned to my computer screen. We tapped away for a few minutes until she exclaimed, "Oh my God you did, didn't you!?"

"What?" I asked, surprised at her outburst.

She glanced over my shoulder. "He just walked into this half of the lab, gave you a really weird look and turned around," she said with disbelief. "You're bloody crazy!" She laughed. I joined in with her laughter, hoping that Jules was out of earshot or he would truly think I was mad.

I asked him out as a joke but inside I wondered what I would have done if he had said yes, if he hadn't been engaged. I would like to say that I would have found some way to get out of it, that I would not seriously consider dating a non-Muslim but I can't. My faith wasn't strong in those days. Yes, I was a Muslim and yes, I did believe in Allah but I was also very angry and used to think that since Allah obviously wasn't protecting me, why should I do all the things I was supposed to and not do the things I wasn't? I knew that if Jules was single and had said yes, I could have gone out with him regardless of the fact that it would have gone against the basis of my religion.

Everything at home was still the same. Things were still going missing. Kamal was still lashing out at everyone when he couldn't scrape together enough cash for a fix. The latest incident had happened when my dad received our phone bill. There had been seventy-eight pounds worth of calls made to a mobile phone alone. I knew instantly that Kamal was responsible for the calls. He did not have his own mobile phone since he could not keep hold of anything of value, opting instead to sell it for a fix. He made on average two phone calls a day from our home phone, talking in murmurs with his dealer and of course, drug dealers don't give out their land-line numbers. After analysing the itemised section, I saw that all the mobile calls were made to just two numbers. My father shook his head at the bill and wondered aloud how he was going to pay it. When I asked him if he was going to say anything to Kamal, he did not respond. As usual, Kamal was allowed to do whatever he wanted and no one said a word.

In order to avoid being at home, I began to spend more time at university. I regularly went home at 7.30 p.m., which was the latest I could get away with. On one of these late evenings, Zahid came and sat next to me.

"You're already doing exam papers?" he asked, glancing over my shoulder at my computer screen.

"God no!" I replied. "I'm just printing them out for the future. I looked at one of these things and it totally freaked me out so I won't be doing that again in the near future."

He smiled but said nothing. His deep dimples lit up his whole face. He was the kind of guy that most girls fell over themselves for but I didn't really find attractive. He was too good-looking for that. I went for a more scruffy and less pretty look.

"So how are you finding the course?" he asked.

"Okay. Most of it is kind of going over my head but Adnan is doing a good job of explaining everything to us."

"Good old Adnan," said Zahid with a hint of sarcasm.

I raised an eyebrow but he said nothing so I turned my attention back to the screen. "What is that you're humming?"

"Oh, come on, you must know it," he replied.

I shook my head.

He whistled the tune but I was still clueless. "It's Airwolf!"

"Oh, right." I threw him a confused look.

"You don't know the theme music to Airwolf?"

"Well, I've heard of it but don't really know what it is."

"Hang on, you've never watched Airwolf?" he asked incredulously.

"Uh, no, not really. I have heard of it and I know it's supposed to be a classic but I've never watched it. What's it about?"

"Wow, well, basically, there's this wolf and he has a gang of guys who have an aeroplane. There's this porn ring which is distributing material and Airwolf and his gang are responsible for tracking them down and stopping them," he explained, animatedly.

"Porn ring? But I thought it was meant to be a kid's programme?"

"It is but it was also programmed for adults," he replied.

"And you knew that it was a porn ring when you used to watch it as a kid?"

He nodded and said, "Yeah, it was pretty obvious."

I shook my head at him. "I'm glad I never watched it then." That's when I saw a slow smile spread across his face and he looked at me cheekily. "You're having me on, aren't you?" I asked.

He burst out laughing and nodded.

"You bastard!" I yelled as he continued to laugh. "I really believed you."

He continued to laugh and said, "Hey, it's not my fault you had a deprived childhood. How can you never have watched Airwolf? That's like saying you never watched 'Nightrider' or 'Thundercats'," he paused, "you *have* seen 'Nightrider' and 'Thundercats' right?"

"Yes, I have!" I narrowed my eyes at him but he simply smiled.

"So why are you here so late anyway?"

"Just. I'm going home soon." I glanced at the clock. It was 7.15 p.m.

"Come on, I'll walk you up."

"No, that's okay," I replied.

"It's dark," he insisted.

"And? As if I've never walked home at this time before."

"Whoah, okay, fair enough," he said. "But when some weirdo grabs you and rapes you, don't blame me."

I looked at him, thinking that that was a dangerous joke but said nothing. "Thanks for the offer Zahid, but honestly, I'm fine."

He shrugged. "Okay, well, I'll see tomorrow," he said and walked off slowly. *Hmm,* I thought, *I like his shirt.*

The music pounded and the lights flashed right into my eyes. I was sweaty, hot and annoyed. No, clubbing *really* wasn't for me. It was seen as an integral part of student life and most students embraced it with open arms but I did not like the drinking, the flirting or the groping that went along with it. I had been persuaded to come out for Ashley's birthday and, despite being a 'convent girl', I had eventually agreed. The mix mainly consisted of Asians. I always knew that Asian Muslims went clubbing with gusto but I never really knew the full extent of what they got up to. There were girls with their cleavages almost inside out grinding up against boys like their lives depended on it. Over made-up faces giggled and laughed madly against the beat of the music. Girls fell over themselves, plied full of alcohol. It really wasn't my scene. Call me boring but I would rather have a nice meal and a movie any day of the week.

I felt a light tap on my shoulder and turned around. It was a tall Pakistani boy that I had been briefly introduced to a week ago.

"Hi Kieran," he said in a Manchester accent.

"Uh, hi," I said, struggling for his name.

"You look nice."

"Thank you."

"I like your top."

"Thank you." I fingered the hem of my black scoop-neck top. The scoop was a little too deep for my liking but its pretty oriental design had caught my eye and Ashley had persuaded me to wear it.

"Would you like to dance?" he shouted over the music as politely as he could.

"Uh, thanks but I'm just keeping an eye on Ashley's drink," I shouted back.

"Hey, you're not one of those who sits in the club all night are you?" he asked.

I laughed and said, "Maybe later!"

One of his friends approached and grabbed him by the shoulders. "Is this scoundrel bothering you, miss?" he asked giddily.

I shook my head.

"Come on Avi man, let's go!" said his friend, dragging him away.

"Thank God," I said under my breath and turned back to my Coke.

A few songs later I spotted Avi dancing with a girl. She was throwing her dyed brown hair into his face and grinding her ass into his crotch. "Classy," I remarked to myself and closed my eyes to relieve the burning headache. I knew then and there that this was to be my first and last clubbing experience.

It's funny how my generation of Asians had such disregard for their religion. Well, actually I should say how *we* had such disregard for *our* religion for I did not pray or wear a headscarf. My defence was that I never disobeyed the rules of my religion through *action* but only through *inaction.* I did not smoke or drink or sleep around. I did not steal or backbite or harm others and in my head, for now, that was doing enough.

It is a stipulation of Islam that parents must do their best to educate their children about Islam and to instil its values in them. My parents used to send us to Arabic classes twice a week but never led by example. Whilst I was growing up, they only prayed in times of severe adversity, not the five times a day they were supposed to. A few of my school friends had a strict religious upbringing and though it occasionally stifled them, I often wished that I had had the same. It bought with it a clarity that I did not have. Allah is what matters and Allah is who we serve. It forces a belief in Allah onto you and I suppose faith was what I had needed during my childhood. As Mr. Bon Jovi so succinctly put it, we all need something to believe in.

A few months into university, Aisha and I were walking down the long spiral stairs from the computer science office. As we stepped out of the tower towards the Informatics Teaching Lab, I spotted Zahid walking towards us.

"Where are you going?" he asked, agitated.

"To the ITL," I replied.

"Don't. Let's have a break. Let's go for a walk or something." His forehead was sweating and he looked really stressed out.

"Is something wrong?" I asked.

"No, let's just walk." We walked through the campus. Students were milling around everywhere laughing and joking but we walked in silence. We reached the canal bank and I turned to him.

"Is something wrong?" I asked again.

"No, it's just that I'm fed up with it all."

"With what?" I asked.

"This. Uni. Everyone is so… so pretentious."

"Pretentious?" I asked. "How do you mean? Everyone I've met seems cool."

"I know… it's just that everyone is trying so hard to be cool and act like they're having fun. Most of them look like they've never had a day of fun in their lives."

He sat down on a wall and shrank inside his oversized jacket. I stood waiting for his outburst to continue. Aisha said nothing also. "Back in the old days, people were genuine. They were real. I don't even know what I'm doing here," he said angrily. I didn't really know what to say. I could hardly say, "Get over yourself and your stupid self-absorbed non-existent problems," which is what I was thinking.

"I mean, all my friends were supposed to be here and I'm the only one who is. And it's the same everywhere. Here, I have to be fake and smile and in East Ham, I walk down the street and everyone is staring at me coz I still haven't been forgiven for it and I have to pretend that I don't care."

"About what?" I asked.

"The accident."

I gave him a confused look.

He took a deep breath and met my eyes. "Remember last Eid, there was a car crash in the Limehouse Link and six boys died?"

I nodded.

"They were my friends and it was my fault," he said.

I heard Aisha gasp quietly next to me. "What happened?" I asked.

"I was supposed to be the responsible one. All their parents looked up to me coz I was the smart one; the one who was gonna make it. 'Stick with him and you'll be alright!'" he said bitterly.

I said nothing.

"I collected them. I collected every single one of them and Faisal's mum didn't want to let him out but I said 'Don't worry Auntie, I promise to have him back before ten' and coz it was me and coz she trusted me, she let him go."

I couldn't understand why Zahid was confiding in us. We had only known him for a few months and usually only spoke to him in passing. I still said nothing.

"We hired out cars and Azarul and I were meant to take care of them. We were in the middle car but we got out." He paused. I could see his lip quivering but I didn't want to ask if he was okay. Sometimes people are fine until someone asks if they are okay and that's when they break down and cry.

"But that doesn't make it your fault," said Aisha.

"Yes it does!" he said. "We got out of the car. We made spaces for the guys in the first car and they were the idiots. They're the ones who convinced Faisul to start racing. They're the ones who goaded him and taunted him and if we had never got out, they would never have got in." He paused. "Do you know how their mothers looked at me? Like I was the dirt underneath their feet. Faisul's mother screamed at me at the funeral. 'Why aren't you there?' she screamed at me. 'You should be dead!' I promised her I would have him back by ten and I left him."

Aisha shook her head but said nothing.

"Six of them. Wiped out, just like that. People say that dead people look like they're sleeping but that's not true. They look dead. There's something about their faces and they look dead."

I looked at the ground. I hurt for him which was unsettling. I never felt sympathy for people I didn't know. I had set my heart in stone so that no one and nothing could affect me emotionally but here I was watching this man shiver in the cold with a distant look in his eye and all I wanted was to hold him and tell him it would be okay.

About one minute after his revelation he stood up, said, "We're late for lecture, let's go!" and popped back into Zahid-the-funny-guy mode. We never spoke about that again but I knew it had affected him badly but that talking to us had helped him for in the following weeks, his smile seemed more genuine and his skin lost its pallor. I didn't know it then but that was the day that I fell in love with him.

Chapter 4. Whitman's Love

"Okay, I'll pick you up at four," I said to James as I dropped him off at the library. The library was not one of our usual haunts but James had started to fall behind on the workload and had decided it was time to sit down and put some hours in. I decided not to sit with him because he would just use me as a distraction, plus I didn't like hanging around in the library. It's funny because even though hanging out in the library is usually a sign of 'nerdiness', at my university it was part of the social scene. Guys and girls stealing fleeting glances at each other, leaning in to whisper in each others' ears, and quiet intimate conversations. It was all used as a pretext to full-on flirting. And me being a 'convent girl', wasn't into it.

On my way out, however, I spotted Zahid sat at a table leaning over a text book. I decided to see if he was okay. As I walked around a cabinet, I saw that he wasn't alone. He was with a table full of girls that I recognised as Avi's friends on the Maths course. One of them was punching him on the shoulder for saying something cheeky. He flashed his dimples at her and she burst into a fit of giggles, flicked her hair and pretended to concentrate on her text book. I decided to leave him at it.

A few days later, I was on the phone to Zahid, asking him about a coursework problem when he suddenly admitted to me that he had started to develop feelings for a girl he knew. I couldn't believe that a smart guy like him had fallen for the girl in the library who I now knew was called Farzana and was apparently famous for turning down guys who asked her out. I knew she wouldn't turn down Zahid. I was dismissive of his confession because I did not want to be privy to his feelings for such an artificial girl but of course, being a man, he did not pick up on my reluctance to discuss her.

"It's stupid, really," he said, "because I haven't been out with a girl since... Well, since the accident and all of a sudden, there are all these stupid feelings for this girl and it feels weird." *Emphasis on the word stupid*, I thought as I listened to him drone on about her.

"For God's sake, Zahid, stop calling her 'this girl'. We both know who you're talking about!" I said in exasperation.

He stopped and asked quietly, "Who?"

"That Farzana girl from Maths."

He was quiet for a moment and then burst out laughing. "You think I would fall for a self-centred, self-righteous, superior, materialistic girl like Farzana who is ashamed of the fact that she's Asian?" he asked in an amused tone.

"I don't know. She seems your type."

"No she's not. She is the polar opposite of my type."

I paused, thinking about how I could be so totally wrong and then the truth dawned on me. "Aisha?" I asked in a disapproving tone. Aisha was indeed the polar opposite of Farzana. She was the quiet to Farzana's brash, she was sweet and humble and always looked for the best in people. I disapproved only because I saw Aisha as being on a pedestal that no man should dare to try and reach and taint with his 'man-ness'.

"No!" replied Zahid, equally as taken aback at the idea that any man should think of pure, sweet Aisha that way.

"Then who?" I asked, stupidly. I could hear his breath quicken.

"It's, uh… it's you," he said simply and shyly. The words struck me like a slap. I had been asked out by guys before but never by one that I considered to be a good friend. I was glad we were on the phone and that he couldn't see the horror on my face.

"Kieran?" he asked quietly. "I'll talk to you tomorrow," and with that he hung up. He had hung up! He could not just drop a bomb like that on me and hang up! I was shocked and flattered and worried. I didn't feel the same way towards him… At least I didn't think I did, plus I wasn't into the whole dating thing. I had never really given boys the time of day and I wasn't about to start now. I needed to concentrate on my studies and also, if my parents found out, which they were bound to, it would be all over for me.

The next day I was approached by Zahid whilst in the library, photocopying a few papers.

"Time away from the fan club?" I asked, beckoning over his shoulder to the table of five girls he'd been sitting with. He said nothing and looked at the floor. Not only was he absolutely gorgeous, he was charming and charismatic. I had seen two sides of him: the dark, brooding, depressed side as well as the funny, charming, cheeky side that women loved so much. Even if I was that way inclined, I would not say yes to this man for I've always maintained that I would never go out with a guy who was prettier than me. A woman needs to feel beautiful.

"How you doing?" he asked.

"I'm okay," I said, fully aware of the five sets of eyes burning holes into me.

"Um, do we need to talk?" he asked.

"You tell me."

He looked me in the eyes. "I think we do."

I nodded. He led me out of the library. The spring air hinted at the winter only just gone by. I wrapped my coat around me tightly as we gravitated towards the canal bank. He turned to me.

"So," I began.

"So," he repeated then took a deep breath. "What are you thinking about what I said yesterday?"

I was the type of girl who never really believed that guys had actually fallen for me. Not because I was insecure but because guys are guys and I believed they never really "fell" for anyone. They were simply attracted to a girl's looks or wanted to take advantage of a comfortable arrangement.

"I think you're confused and that what you said yesterday was something you'll probably regret in a week or so."

He raised an eyebrow. "You really think that?"

"Yes." I met his gaze as he shook his head.

"You're so wrong. Kieran, I haven't gone out with a girl for three years. I haven't even *thought* about girls for three years. Ever since the accident, I just couldn't be bothered with it... with anything. So believe me when I say that I meant it."

I didn't really know what to say so said nothing.

"Kieran, I want to be with you," he said.

"Why me?" I asked. I was genuinely confused as to why he would choose me. He could have his pick of girls at uni.

"Because I've never met anyone like you. Because you're smart. Because you have things going on in here," he gestured to his head. "You're independent, you're strong. You know exactly where you're going. You're together," he paused, "and you're beautiful."

I was taken aback by how genuine his words were. I was so flattered but I knew that I could not say yes to him for so many reasons. I took a step back and looked down.

He shook his head and said nothing.

"Zahid, I… I'm very flattered but I can't."

"Why not?"

"I don't date."

"Everybody dates."

I raised an eyebrow at him.

"Why don't you date?" he asked.

"Why *do* you date?" I asked.

"I don't."

"Everybody dates," I said back to him.

He smiled wryly. "Okay," he said finally. "But I'm not giving up," and with that he turned around and walked away.

I sat on the canal wall and picked up a pebble. *Shit! What the hell is going on?* I was extremely flattered that someone like Zahid was attracted to me and I really enjoyed being with him but there was no way anything could happen. Even if we tried our best to keep it under wraps, I knew my parents would find out somehow. Don't get me wrong, I like being Asian. I like having two different cultures. Coming from an Asian background gives you an automatic affinity with other Asian youth, like you're a part of a secret society, one where guys and girls mix and date in abundance which our parents would be horrified by. For example, if I saw a guy that I knew with a girl, I would not tell my parents or spread it around and I like to think he would do the same for me. Maybe it was a false sense of affinity but somehow it made us feel safe. And that's how my subconscious slowly started to convince me to say yes to Zahid. I got up, threw the pebble into the water and walked off to my lecture.

"You're kidding, right?" said Ashley, chewing the end of her pencil.

"Nope," I replied, puzzling over my text book.

"But how can the bastard expect us to learn concurrency as well? It's two bloody chapters in the book!"

I nodded.

"I'm not doing it," she said.

"Ashley, you have to."

"Nope, I'm going for a coffee and if I fail this exam, then I fail it. We have only got one week until the exams start and I can't afford to abandon everything else for this one exam. I'm being sensible." With that she gathered her belongings and left with flourish.

I shook my head and went back to my book. I couldn't concentrate. I hated working in the library but I couldn't study at home and where else was there? I had tried to find empty rooms to study in but sooner or later there would be some revision class or meeting there and I would waste more time relocating so I had given in and come to the library. Ashley and I had sat together but the rest of us had disbanded in the hope that we would get more done if we were alone. On the contrary, I was struggling with ideas I couldn't understand.

"Problems?" asked a voice, quietly.

I looked up to see Zahid. He had a habit of always turning up when I needed someone. I nodded and he leaned down next to me.

"What's wrong?"

"Bloody semaphores. I still can't get my head around them," I answered.

He pulled out the chair next to me and sat down. "What's confusing?" he asked.

"I don't understand the difference between a monitor and a semaphore. I know they're both used for message passing but how are they different?"

He ripped a piece of paper from my pad and drew a diagram, whispering the explanation to me. His proximity made me feel hot all of a sudden. I bit my lip and tried to ignore the faint sense of excitement. I stared blankly at the diagram, nodding.

Three months had passed since he'd confessed his feelings to me. Things had fluctuated from being awkward to totally comfortable between us. There were times I would catch his eye and look away quickly but others when we would let our eyes linger with meaning and understanding. He asked me to reconsider frequently but I always resisted.

He brushed my arm as he was explaining the diagram and I saw his intake of breath. He turned to me, his lips close to mine and we froze for a second. I cleared my throat and quickly thanked him for helping me.

"Any time," he said. He looked me straight in the eyes for a few seconds and then got up and left. I caught my breath and tried to get back to my work.

That evening, after dinner, I tried to get down to a bit of revision. I couldn't get my head into it so decided to have a break and call my best friend, Rabika, instead. I had my own land-line, which I used mainly for the internet, so I could usually chat to whomever I wanted with a bit of privacy, which was impossible when using the home phone. Rabika and I had chatted together yesterday but were cut short because I had to go and make a phone call for my father.

I pressed re-dial on my phone and heard a man's voice say, "Hello?"

"Uh, hello? May I speak to Rabika please?" I checked the number.

"Who?"

"I'm sorry, I've got the wrong number," I replied as I realised that the dialled number wasn't Rabika's number. I tried to think if I had called anyone after I spoke to her yesterday but knew that I hadn't. I pressed redial again so I could copy down the number and then hung up before it started to ring. The number looked familiar. I keyed it into my mobile phone and dialled to see if there was anyone in my phone book with that number but there wasn't. I wracked my brains, convinced that I had seen the number somewhere before. It hit me all at once. I ran downstairs and opened the phone bill I had scoured a few weeks before. Sure enough, the mobile number on the itemised bill matched the one I had noted down.

"Ama!" I yelled, calling my mother.

"What?" she called back from the living room.

"He's been in my room!" I yelled with cheeks red from anger.

"Who?"

"Who else!?" I yelled. "He used my phone. He's been calling a mobile with my landline."

"How do you know?" she asked, barely glancing in my direction.

"I was calling a friend and I pressed redial on the phone and it went to a mobile phone and some guy answered."

"Well, perhaps you dialled wrong yesterday," she replied.

"No, I didn't. I spoke to Rabika yesterday. I haven't called anyone since then. The number matches the one on the phone bill."

"Don't worry. I'll tell him not to use your phone without asking," she said dismissively.

"Is that all you're gonna say? He's racked up SEVENTY EIGHT pounds on our home phone bill. God only knows how much he's racked up on mine! Why was he in my room anyway? Why is he using my phone? Does he pay the bill?" I yelled but my mother turned away.

I stormed upstairs. "That bastard better not use my phone again!" I shouted at the top of my voice not caring if he heard, actually wanting him to hear. How dare he come into my room and touch my things?

Kamal was in the bathroom and came out. "Oi, you stupid idiot!" he yelled. "It was a two second call! It cost ten fucking pence."

"What the hell were you doing in my room? And ten pence adds up when you make hundreds of calls!"

"I'll throw that money in your face you fucking bitch," he screamed at me. His face was gaunt and tight with anger. His eyes had nearly popped out of their sockets but his hollow cheeks remained colourless. Years of drug-taking had moulded his face into what looked like a skull. His tall skinny frame walked towards me angrily but I had fire in my eyes and I wasn't backing down.

"Why the hell are you using it for in the first place? All you do is take money from Mum and Dad and then sniff it all up your nose. Don't use my phone again!"

That's what made him lose the plot. He started running up the stairs for me. "It was ten fucking pence, you stupid bitch!"

"Kieran!" screamed Sania from the top of the stairs. I ran up the last flight of stairs as quickly as I could and slammed my door shut just as Sania slammed hers. I locked it quickly as I heard my father chase him up the stairs.

"What are you doing?" said my father. "Come downstairs. If you need to use the phone, just use the house phone."

There was no stopping him though. He went downstairs in a rage. My father made a single comment to him about not coming into my room and he lost it. He smashed the kitchen up. He kicked the fridge, making a dent in it and then threw all my mother's curries against the walls. He was crazed. I mean *really* crazed. When a person is in that state, there is no getting through to them. He yelled obscenities at me and my father for about ten minutes and then stormed out of the house.

My sisters and I spent two hours cleaning the curry off the white walls.

The exam period came and went and my first year at university was over so quickly, it felt like it hadn't even begun. I didn't tell my parents when I finished my last exam because not having to go to uni meant not having to go out at all and I wasn't ready to give up my freedom for four months. I went to uni anyway and sat at a computer and just messed around. On a few of these occasions, some of the people on my course would be in uni collecting exam results or asking their personal tutors for job references and they would pop into the ITL. "What are you doing here?" they would ask. "It's the holidays! Go home!" I simply asked them the same question and went back to my work.

They didn't know that staying at home was like suffocating slowly and that the cold granite ITL was better. I did go out alone - shopping, eating and even to the movies - but I always ended up in the ITL. One morning, I was walking to uni, extra depressed. I didn't want to be in the ITL with nothing to do all day but I wanted to be at home even less. At that precise moment, my phone rang. It was Zahid.

"Hello?" I said.

"Hi," he said. I felt a sudden rush of excitement. It had been two weeks since uni had finished and I hadn't spoken to him since. "How are you?" he asked.

"I'm okay," I replied.

"Where are you?" he asked as a car zoomed by.

"I'm just going shopping," I lied. We talked for a while before he asked me if I wanted to meet up with him 'just as friends'. I didn't want to lead him on so I said no but he persisted. I had felt so lonely during the past two weeks that I desperately needed some company. Time spent with Zahid was always warm and pleasant and indulging… so I agreed.

"Great!" he yelled, then coughed to subdue his obvious delight. I smiled at his reaction. I loved feeling wanted.

We met at Surrey Quays underground station and walked towards Pizza Hut. The meal was lovely and intimate. We talked about everything from the East End's drug problem to whether Michael Jackson was innocent or not. We ate lots and laughed hard. When it was finished, I didn't want to leave him. He suggested going to watch a movie. I wanted to say no, I wanted to tell him to back off but I couldn't. I sat next to him in the cinema nervously. Our eyes met during the movie several times and I could see he was contemplating whether or not he should touch my hand or move closer. He did neither, which was a relief but a tiny part of me deep inside also felt disappointed. After the movie, we decided to go for a walk along Canary Wharf. There, he finally turned to me and asked if he could kiss me. I leaned forward and his lips met mine. Now I know people say they feel butterflies in their stomach but this was more like a stampede. My lips tingled from his gentle kiss as I stepped back breathlessly. *This stuff is only meant to happen in the movies*. Our eyes met and I could see that he was fighting a smile.

"What?" I asked, softly.

He shook his head and silently wrapped his arms around me. I think that was the first time in my life that I felt truly safe and truly protected. I can't describe what it felt like without drawing from every cliché in the so-called book. I pushed back any negative thought and simply revelled in the moment. When he finally let go, I didn't know how to react. We had known each other for nearly a year; we were close friends who were extremely comfortable with each other but the small part of our relationship that hinted at more had finally become a realisation and now it was different. He solved my dilemma by leaning in for another kiss. And that, I suppose, sealed the deal.

Zahid and I saw as much of each other as we could during the holidays. I eventually had to tell my parents that uni had finished because I did not want them to get suspicious. Spending those five weeks apart was difficult. So difficult in fact that it started to freak me out. I had never felt this way about someone before and part of me really didn't like it. I was used to being independent so becoming emotionally reliant on someone else was disconcerting. I suppressed these feelings and tried to just enjoy being with him. We had long phone conversations deep into the night. It was crazy because I had always been a girl who couldn't stand the thought of calling her boyfriend everyday. *How much could you tell him today that you didn't tell him yesterday?* I had always thought but all of that had changed now. I loved talking to him. I could tell him anything and everything, and I did. I told him about Kamal's drug habit, about how much I despised my mother, about how I always felt trapped. He understood and sympathised and soothed me. He became my rock. That summer was blissful and probably the happiest of our relationship. My second year of university started and with it came new hopes, new fears and new problems.

Zahid and I had decided to keep our relationship secret. I knew of many couples at uni but none who dated openly. Well, not any Muslim couples anyway. It just wasn't the done thing. I found it amusing how guys and girls went clubbing and drinking yet refused to admit that they were dating. It was a big taboo that neither Zahid nor I were willing to break. I was already seen as 'sinful' because I did not wear a headscarf and socialised openly with members of the opposite sex. In fact, one Muslim boy went so far as to call me a 'part-time Muslim' behind my back during Ramadan. I was fasting, as is required in Islam for the month of Ramadan and when this boy, Akbur, learnt of this, he was 'disgraced' since I did not adhere to the rest of the rules of Islam and apparently, I *chose* only to do so during Ramadan.

I can't describe the fury I felt when I heard this. I am a strong believer that you should not pass judgement on others if you are not faultless yourself. Like the old adage, *Let he who is without sin cast the first stone* dictates, if you have done wrong in your life, you should not look at others and speak wrong of them. Firstly, just by saying what he did, he was indulging in backbiting and gossip which is a punishable sin in Islam. He and his kind assume that just because a girl wears a headscarf or *hijab*, she is pure and innocent and as good as gold. BULLSHIT. It made me so angry how men felt they could judge a woman by how much of her hair they could see. It was okay for them to roam around doing just as they pleased but if they saw a woman without her head covered, she was a *part-time Muslim.* Akbur was highly competitive and periodically lied about how well he was getting on with the course just to avoid helping others. Was this Islamic? Was that praiseworthy? I am not the model Muslim woman; I know that and accept it but I do not pretend that I am perfect. I do not pretend that I am without sin just so I can speak badly of others. I will wear the scarf when I am good and ready, not because some self-righteous, self-centred, stuck-up hypocrite insists that I should. Why was I affecting him anyway? Superior Muslim men are afraid of self-confident attractive Muslim women and *that's* what it was. But as is the norm for good Bengali women, I did not confront him. Instead, I simply gritted my teeth and moved on.

On a cold September Tuesday, a few days after uni had started again, I yawned and forced myself out of bed. I wrapped my oversized GAP zip-up top around me and shivered. I debated whether to go into uni and loaf around until my 3 p.m. lecture or stay at home and leave thirty minutes before it. I hated being at home but the thought of another lonely morning in the ITL was enough to drive me crazy. I decided to spend the morning at home.

A few hours later, I gathered the clothes I needed to iron for the day. As I stepped out, I heard the television blaring downstairs. *Who the hell?* I thought to myself. Only Neha listened to the TV that loud and she was still asleep despite it being almost 2 p.m.

I walked downstairs to find my father with his eyes glued to the screen.

"What's happening?" I enquired.

My dad pointed the television. "The buildings. They have collapsed," he said blankly.

"What buildings?" I looked at the T.V. He was watching the news. I listened to what the reporter was saying.

"... collapsed within thirty minutes of the first. Its fate was the same as the South Tower; American Airlines Flight 11 flew straight into the North Tower at exactly 8.46 a.m. Eastern Daylight Time and 12.53 p.m. GMT, just as American workers were getting to their desks. It is... "

"What's going on?" I asked my father.

"Ssh!" he hissed.

I turned my concentration on the report.

"... desperately jumping out of windows up to thirty stories high. All local buildings and businesses were destroyed by the blast. The accuracy and synchronistic nature of this tragedy indicates that this is an act of terrorism. The White House and the Capitol have been evacuated amid

further threats. All airports across the US have been shut down and all commercial flights have been grounded. We can now show you images of the events. Please be warned that some viewers may be disturbed by the following images... "

The reporter's voice was superimposed on a picture of the twin towers in New York City. Only they were not the twin towers because there was only one tower there. Instead of the other, there was a gaping space. The remaining tower was burning out of control. There was an aircraft lodged right into the centre of the building, forming a surreal and demonic tableau.

"Oh, my God!" I said when I realised that the small ant-like figures falling from the building to the ground were people. "Oh my God! How did this happen?" I turned to my father.

He continued to watch the screen. Suddenly, the building crumpled and buckled then rushed to the ground in one fell swoop, leaving behind an enormous cloud of dust and fumes. I could not believe what I was seeing. I could not understand it.

"*... changing the New York skyline forever...* " I blinked and tried to hear what the reporter was saying. *How the hell did this happen?* I thought. I switched channels and the same report was everywhere. We watched more footage of the buildings crashing down and heard people at the scene give shaken accounts of their first-hand experiences.

"Was it planned?" I asked my father.

"That is what they are saying."

"Well, who did it?"

"I don't know. The CIA has said that it is definitely a terrorist organisation. They are trying to find out who was flying the plane and what happened."

"But surely they *know* who was flying the plane. It was an American Airlines plane, the woman said. Can't they just look it up?"

"They suspect that the plane was hijacked," he said.

"What? Hijacked by whom?" I asked, getting flashbacks of Die Hard 2. I shook my head. This was real life, not some action movie. "But if it was hijacked, how did they get out of the plane? They won't have just flown straight into a building."

"They are calling it a suicide mission." My father spoke the words that

I would go on to hear many more times in my life.

"A suicide mission? But what kind of crazy people would go and do something like that?"

"They are saying that it was an Islamic organisation."

I stopped dead. "What Islamic organisation? What are they talking about?"

"I'm not sure yet. But that is what they are saying."

"But... Where the hell are they getting this information from? Why on earth would we do something like that?"

"I don't know but I'm sure we will find out."

I ran upstairs and called Zahid. "Are you watching what happened?" I asked.

"Yes," he answered grimly.

"What's going on?"

"Some people are saying that it's Al-Qaeda, an Islamic group lead by Osama Bin Laden."

"I know who that is! He's number one the FBI's most wanted list."

"How did you know that?"

"Oh, Javed came round that one time and he was checking random stuff on my PC, you know what he's like, and he was looking at the top ten most wanted list and he told me about that guy."

"What did he say?"

"That's he's Afghani and he's wanted for all these bombings and stuff. Isn't it all a little neat to blame it on him?"

"I don't know, Kieran. I'm still watching the news. They don't know what the hell happened."

"But why would Al-Qaeda do that?"

"Because they hate America."

"Why?"

"Why not? You know what America is like. They think they're above all other nations in the world. They think they're superior."

"But that's no reason to do what they did."

"Of course it isn't but America is backing the Jews in Palestine and not the Muslims so there's obviously a great deal of hate and anger towards them in the Muslim community."

"So you really think that's what happened? That some Islamic organisation did this?"

"It's a possibility."

"But how can they possibly justify killing all those people? And suicide no less! If someone is dedicated enough to want to kill others for Islam, then how can they justify committing suicide? It's one of the greatest sins in Islam!"

"I know, Kieran. But they're not normal Muslims are they? They're extremists. They have strong ideas and they act on those ideas rather than talk about them all day."

"But I don't understand. How could this happen? I mean, with security and stuff, how could it?"

"It was a domestic flight. Security is much more lax than on an international flight."

"But still. I'm assuming these men had guns or knives or some sort of weapons. How did they get on the plane?"

"I don't know."

"But all those people! There must have been thousands in those buildings!"

"I know."

"So you *really* think that Muslims could have done this?"

"I hope not, Kieran. The media reporting it that way is bad enough."

"Well, what are they basing all this on?"

"I don't know but it's going to be a bad time for Muslims. A really bad time."

Looking back, it strikes me how quick I was to place myself in the same category as those suspected of the terrorist acts. "Why on earth would *we* do something like that?" I had asked my father. Could I really blame the world's media and the public for dumping us all in the same category when I had been all too willing to do so myself? Just as Zahid had predicted, 9/11 was not good publicity for Muslims. It created a palpable tension between us and the rest of the world.

I know that there is a general animosity between Asians of different religions but I had never felt it. To me, we were all Asians in a predominantly white country and we stuck together. 9/11 changed all that. Sikhs and Hindus became sick of being banded together with Muslims. They became sick of being harassed in the street by youths who didn't really know anything about Islam or politics. They were not to blame for what had happened but then neither were we.

Was I, as a Muslim woman, responsible for the attacks on the twin towers? No, I was not. So how come I was harassed on the bus on my way to Rayya's house in Leyton? How come I was asked the classic question, "Why don't you go back to where you came from?" How come my best friend was called "Osama Bin Laden's daughter" just because she expressed her right to wear a headscarf? How come my father had to endure a tirade from a white man at a bus stop?

I had to deal with the racist issues of white people but more importantly, I had to deal with racist issues within myself. I had never thought of myself as a racist person but after experiencing the reactions of white Britons to 9/11, I could not stop certain thoughts. After listening to yet another middle-aged white woman, dressed in tracksuit bottoms with a cigarette in one hand, denounce Muslims and Islam and people of all ethnic minorities, I could not help but think, "Stupid white woman." But the scary thing was, it was not just uneducated, unemployed white people who had these ideas and opinions. It was also clear thinking, educated men and women. They banded all Muslims in the same category and that's what pissed me off the most. They saw us as these beasts with primitive customs and outdated ideas that ought to be sent back to the countries we originated from. *If this is how bad it is in London, imagine what it's like in America,* I thought.

I also wondered about Osama Bin Laden and his band of men. What had they been thinking? I know they had a vendetta against America and they had obviously thought their plans through very carefully, but what were they thinking? The media bandied around the word *jihad* which truthfully, was the only explanation. *Jihad* literally translates as 'struggle' in Arabic. Among conservative Muslims, the word had come to mean 'holy war'. These men thought they were fighting a holy war, one that was forged in the name of Allah, and therefore that they would be highly rewarded for their actions. Any man or woman that fights in *jihad* gets a reward of eternal paradise.

Of course, before you engage in war, it has to be officially declared as *jihad*. But as there is currently no single established authority governing the Muslim world, the only de-facto Islamic leaders are the governments of the modern Muslim states. However, due to the allegiance and subservience of many Middle Eastern states to the world's non-Islamic superpowers such as America, extremists believe that the modern Muslim states are un-Islamic. As a result, Islamic groups such as Al-Qaeda took the initiative to declare jihad, bypassing the authority of their state, which ultimately resulted in 9/11.

The events of 9/11 created a spirit of 'Us' and 'Them', with the USA on one side and Al Qaeda and Muslims on the other. In truth, most Muslims were stuck somewhere in the middle, just praying that things would get better. I thanked my lucky stars that I lived in an area with a high concentration of Muslims and went on living in my cocoon. What else was there to do?

Chapter 5. Breathing Space

As my second year of university drew on, Zahid and I became closer but growing intimacy bought growing problems. We finally had the 'exes-conversation' - the dreaded conversation that all couples have about the number of ex-partners/serious relationships/etc they have had. When pursuing me, Zahid had said that he hadn't dated for three years so naturally I assumed that he hadn't had many partners. I knew he was not a pure and innocent virgin. Looking like he did, he probably had to fight them off through school but I wasn't quite ready for what he had to reveal.

Zahid had attended a mixed school and boy, had he mixed! He had had three proper girlfriends and countless 'encounters' with girls at his school. He had started work at SegaWorld, a big entertainment/arcade complex in Leicester Square, in the heart of London, the week he turned sixteen and there he found girls galore. I was surprised at his candidness when he told me that he had probably been with nearly thirty girls at SegaWorld. Now, when I say 'been with', I do not necessarily mean 'had sex with', I mean 'had sexual encounters with' but that was bad enough. I couldn't believe what I was hearing. I knew guys went a bit sex-mad through puberty but this was just taking the piss. I didn't really know what to think. Here I was, a girl who had abstained from any contact with members of the opposite sex over the past five years while he had indulged in every opportunity that had come his way. I had a quick flashback to Akbur shaking Zahid's hand with an Asalam Alaikum. Funny how Muslim men are not judged by their appearance whereas it's the *only* thing women are judged on.

I felt slightly sick after hearing what he had to say. Part of me wished he hadn't been so honest; ignorance is bliss and all of that but I was glad he had. Even so, I wasn't about to commend him for his honesty. When he finished confessing his many, *many* sins, he asked if I was okay.

"Yes," I replied after a moment's silence.

"Kieran, I'm being honest with you because I'm serious about you. I don't want to lie to you." His words didn't make me feel any better. Even in Western culture, a woman would balk at hearing that her partner had had nearly thirty sexual escapades. In our culture, it was incomprehensible. I'm not a traditionalist and I'm not blind to the things that go on in modern Asian culture but this was just a little too much.

"Zahid, I'll talk to you tomorrow," I said quickly and hung up before he had a chance to protest. I really didn't know how to feel. I wasn't angry at him because it wasn't like he had cheated on me. I wasn't sad or upset… I suppose I was just shocked. Immediately, my imagination ran into overdrive imagining all these stunning women and what they had done with him. Actually, scratch the part where I said I wasn't angry because the more I thought about it, the angrier I became. It was so goddamned typical. So bloody typical that I would go for a guy who was a complete whore. *What did you expect?* asked a little voice inside me. *Just look at him.* I should have known better than to really believe that a guy like Zahid would seriously be interested in me. Don't get me wrong, I'm not Medusa or anything. I've never been a stranger to the affections and advances of men but at the same time, I had never been the most beautiful girl in class either and I was certainly not on a par with Zahid. My petite seven stones stood at 5'1" and my mixture of long black hair, brown eyes and fair skin was really nothing to write home about.

Zahid called me back immediately after I hung up but I didn't want to talk to him just yet. I needed to sort things out in my head. I ignored his call and went downstairs to get something to eat.

As I entered the kitchen, I heard Kamal ask my Dad for twenty pounds, which of course was given to him despite the fact that he had taken another ten from him earlier. I shook my head but said nothing. I tried not to think about it because every time I did, it made me so angry. My parents knew they were feeding his drug habit with money they couldn't afford to give away and yet they did it anyway. I wasn't in the mood to worry about it so I just grabbed a packet of crisps and retired to my room.

I checked my phone: four missed calls. I threw it back onto my bed and ignored it. I put some music on and sat on my floor in silence. The second year exams were three months away and I wasn't ready for them. I let the depression wash over me. I wanted to get out of this life. I wanted to be free of my parents, free of my culture, free of this unrelenting feeling of unfulfilment. I don't want to sound like one of Kerouac's restless anti-heroes who had so much but failed to recognise it. I don't want to be one of those people who moan about how depressed they are when they have very little to be depressed about, but I couldn't help it. I felt like giving up on it all. Zahid had breathed a bit of fresh air into my life and now he too, was fuelling my problems. I hadn't slept with him yet but at the same time, our relationship wasn't completely innocent either. I had let him touch me and now, to learn that he had been with so many others, I felt dirty. I felt *filthy.* I changed into my pyjamas and crept into my bed. I didn't want to face the world in the morning. I just wanted to sleep and sleep and sleep.

The next day, Zahid approached me as I sat in front of a computer in the ITL tapping away mindlessly.

"Kieran," he said softly. I turned to face him.

"Hi," I said quietly.

"Listen, we obviously need to talk. I'm gonna go and you follow me in about five minutes. I'll meet you, top floor of the CS building."

I wasn't in the mood to talk to him but I wasn't in the mood to argue either so I nodded.

As he left, Ashley came and sat next to me. "Is there something going on between you two?" she asked, cutting straight to the chase.

I tried to look surprised. "Me and Zahid?" I asked. "Don't be silly."

"I'm not being silly. I've seen the way you look at each other and the way you always sit so close. What's going on?"

"Really, nothing is going on. As if a guy like that would go for a girl like me."

"Whatever you say," she said and walked off, smiling.

I got up too and went to meet Zahid. As I stepped onto the landing of the top floor of the Computer Science building, I could see his silhouette. He faced a large window, both arms stretched out, supporting himself against the glass. I tapped him on the shoulder and he jumped as he turned around.

"Are you okay?" he asked.

I nodded.

"What are you thinking?"

"I don't know."

"You don't know? Come on Kieran. I need you to talk to me about this."

"I don't know what to think, Zahid. So you were a tart, what can I do about it?"

"You can tell me how much of a problem this is going to be."

"I don't know, okay? I want to say 'Hey, it's all cool' but I'm just having a hard time taking it all in. I mean, you tell me you've been with twenty-seven girls or however many there were, and what - I'm supposed to just accept it and move on?"

"Kieran, I don't want this to be a problem. I told you because I wanted us to have a clean start. Should I have lied to you?" he asked with smouldering dark eyes. He ran a hand through his hair and looked me in the eyes. "Kieran, I know it doesn't mean a lot to you but I put myself on the line for you. I've never gone after a girl the way I did with you. I've never cared about a girl the way I care for you. It's all in the past now. Let's just forget it and move on," he pleaded.

What was I supposed to say to that? I couldn't say no and I couldn't say yes. I was angry and hurt by it but at the same time, he was right: it *was* all in the past and he did care about me. I could see that. And I knew I was falling in love with him. Here was this amazing, gorgeous, smart, funny guy who wanted me. I couldn't let this get in the way. I nodded and he laughed out loud with relief. He reached out and scooped me into his arms.

"Kieran, I swear you're not gonna regret this." He kissed my hair. I felt so safe in his arms. I snuggled into his chest and breathed him in. He held me tight and kissed me until I felt the stirrings of his hard-on.

I shook my head at him. "How can you think of something like that after what we've just talked about?"

He smiled that smile of his that made you forget everything and simply leaned in to kiss me.

As the second year exams drew closer, problems at home got worse. Kamal had started to knock on the doors of neighbours and ask for money. This is something that is shameful in any culture but unbearably so in ours. I always became angry with my father for being Kamal's endless bank supply. My father hadn't given him any money for a few days and obviously he had now found an ingenious way of making my father pay. I felt trapped and powerless. Being passive was not in my nature and having to deal with a situation which I could not do anything about was eating away at me. I had fantasies about hiring a hit man to kill my brother. I know that sounds heartless but I meant it. If he died, I would not feel an ounce of sorrow. In fact, I may be inclined to organise a celebration.

If I was a 'normal' person who heard that someone had a drug addict in their family, I would probably think, *Okay, that's bad luck. I hope he gets better*, and I probably wouldn't understand the enormity of it, of how much it affects the other members of the family. We lived in a house where nothing was safe; not our possessions, not our emotions, not our space and time. We locked our doors when we went out, we now locked our doors when we went downstairs to eat, and we locked our doors when we went to the goddammned toilet. This is what we had to do because any complacency would mean your mobile phone would be missing the next day, or your mini-disc player, or twenty pounds from your purse. We couldn't relax because we didn't know when he would have one of his outbursts. He had such disregard for the consequences of his actions.

I know drug addiction is looked upon by professionals as a disease, something that addicts can't help. It means that they're sick and they deserve sympathy etc, etc. You know what I have to say to that? Bullshit. It's all bullshit. I don't care how bad people have it or how they got into it; they are stupid weak fuckers who should sort themselves out.

I know I sound ignorant but when you have watched your little sisters get beaten up time and time again, when you have watched your sixty-five year old father cower under his twenty-five year old son's raised fist, when you have watched your family being slowly ripped apart, you couldn't be blamed for having no sympathy. And I meant it when I said I wished he was dead.

Despite problems at home, I got through the exams and entered the holidays with a mixture of relief and apprehension. I was glad that the pressure of the exams was off but I didn't want to spend four months at home. Like last year, I didn't tell my parents that uni had finished until six weeks into the holiday. I saw Zahid a lot but of course, he couldn't spend every day of six weeks with me. I sat in the ITL on my own just surfing the net. The few days I went out with Zahid were good but at the same time, I could see myself becoming this person I didn't want to be.

Every time we walked past a pretty girl, I became paranoid. I was never the type of girl who bristled in the presence of an attractive female. There were girls who hated other girls simply because they were prettier but I had never been like that. I was secure in my skin and had never been the jealous type. Now that I knew what Zahid had been like, I couldn't help myself. He was a flirt, I knew that from watching him with the girls in the library and I couldn't help but feel inferior to all the stunning girls he had been out with in the past. I picked fights with him out of insecurity and gradually it became so bad that we were having arguments nearly every night.

One night, we were in the middle of a particularly bad argument. He had cancelled his plans with me in favour of a birthday celebration with his best friend Tasneem, his *female* friend Tasneem. Apparently, they had known each other since they were about thirteen and she was the closest thing to him, ever. He had told me about how she was there for him during the accident involving the death of his friends and how she helped him through it. He talked about how she was 'so different' from other girls and how he was completely comfortable with her. I instantly felt angry and jealous. He reiterated that I had nothing to be jealous about and that they were just platonic friends, nothing more, nothing less, but I could not help it. And now he was cancelling plans with me for her. I was absolutely livid. I had begged him to introduce me to her. *Better the devil you know* and all that but he flat out refused saying that he could not let anyone from his area know that he was going out with someone because it could get back to his family.

"I can't believe you, Zahid," I yelled at him. "You're always so busy and this one time I can come out, you cancel on me for *her*."

"Kieran, listen, I can see you any time. I haven't seen her for almost a year now."

"But that's just the thing, Zahid! You can't see me any time. You think it's easy for me to make up an excuse every time I come out and see you? You think it's just a matter of 'Oh Mum, I'm going out…'? My parents aren't as liberal as yours or Tasneem's! I can't believe you're going to cancel on me for her!"

"Kieran, fine, I won't go."

"No, I'm not asking you not to go. I'm just saying I can't believe you want to."

"I won't go. I wasn't telling you that I was cancelling on you, I was asking you."

"Fine Zahid! Go! Do what you want!" I screamed. I was so angry I could feel hot tears well up in my eyes. *I'm not going to cry.*

"I'm not going to go, okay?" he said calmly.

"So, what? Now you're gonna call her and tell her how the 'evil jealous girlfriend' won't let you come?"

"No, she doesn't know about you, remember?" he said quietly.

"Oh, that's right! You can't tell her coz it would get back to your family. I don't get it. You bang on about how much you trust her, then why can't you trust her to keep this to herself? It's not that you *can't* tell her, it's that you don't *want* to!"

"Kieran, please… "

"What? What do you want?"

"Come away with me."

"What!?"

"Come away with me. We can go away for a while. Get away from London, this life and what we've become."

"What do you mean 'what we've become'? If you don't like what we've become, why don't we just forget about it?" I tried to draw him back into the argument. I don't know why I did it but I couldn't help myself.

"Kieran, sssh," he said gently. "I love you and I want to be with you. Somewhere far away where we can be alone and just enjoy being together."

"No… " I started.

"This isn't you, Kieran. You're not this girl who goes mad over small things. You're crazy and sweet and smart. Let's forget about Tasneem. I want to go away with you. Please."

I loved him so much and I hated the person I had become. Maybe he was right, maybe we did need to get away and remember what it was like when we had first got together. It had only been a year since we had started going out and already it felt like cracks were beginning to show. I was so in love with him but I magnified every little thing he said that hurt me and turned it into a colossal argument. I knew on some level, I was messed up. I couldn't accept being happy with him. I freaked out when I got too happy but I knew he was right. I agreed and we began to plan how to get around my parents. Eventually, we decided on a two-week break to Tunisia. I lied to my parents and said it was a school trip (with my old single sex school). I don't know if they fell for it but after much persuasion, they agreed to let me go.

A few weeks later, Zahid and I set off to the airport, filled with hope and excitement. As we landed in the Tunisian airport, I gripped his hand hard. I was so excited and filled with anticipation. I had vowed to myself that I wouldn't act like the jealous girlfriend that I had become, and that we would have a good time together. The hotel was beautiful. It had an earthy, musty, smell which reminded him of Pakistan and me of Bangladesh. This difference was something I often forgot: Zahid was Pakistani, not Bengali like me. For such a big obstacle, it was surprising how easily I forgot about it. Dating outside your community is a big no-no. Zahid and I were extremely serious about each other but we both knew that when it came to crunch-time and marriage, the fact that we were from different countries and backgrounds would be an insurmountable problem. If he was Bengali like me, maybe, just maybe, we could have faced our parents over it. I knew of a handful of girls who had a love marriage, which was passed off as an arranged marriage by their parents in order to save face. In our case, there was no way my parents could pretend that it was an arranged, 'honourable', marriage. Cross-cultural arranged marriages just did not happen. What it boiled down to was just good old-fashioned racism. Under Islam, all Muslims were equal; no type of Muslim was more worthy than another. In reality however, it was very different. My parents would sooner kill me than let me marry a Pakistani boy. I had thought about all this when I had initially resisted Zahid's advances but it was his smile and his eyes and all the things that make you fall in love that melted away all my reservations. I didn't know what the future would bring. I just wanted to enjoy my time with him.

Our room had a huge bed in it and was furnished with a small kitchen, two sofas and a television. We dropped onto the bed in an exhausted heap. It was 10 p.m. local time and we were both starving. We filled up on some snacks and once we had showered, fell into a deep sleep in each other's arms.

The next morning I was roused by the gentle sound of waves. I stirred and then slowly woke up. Zahid wasn't next to me. I threw back the light duvet, sat up and spotted him out on the balcony. I padded over to him and he smiled.

"Look." He pointed out past the balcony.

I gasped. The sea was blue just like in holiday brochures and adverts. Last night, when we had settled down, we couldn't see the sea because of the darkness and had just assumed that the buildings gave way to empty ground but it was a glorious blue sea. I laughed with delight and Zahid wrapped me up in his arms. He kissed my cheek and held me tightly. I sighed contently and snuggled into his warmth.

That day, we checked out the beach (beautiful), the food (delicious) and the locals (lovely) and just enjoyed talking. By the time we got back to our apartment, we were both drunk on the moonlight and the sounds of the sea. He leaned in and kissed me. I felt the stirrings of his hard-on and smiled quietly. We hadn't had sex yet, for a number of reasons. First and foremost, we were Muslim and it just wasn't the done thing and secondly, because I was scared about it. I leaned into him and breathed him in. He kissed me hard and laid me down on the bed. He undressed me quickly and began to kiss me all over. He trailed a path of kisses down my stomach and began to kiss and lick me. I moaned with pleasure at the feeling of his tongue against me.

"Mmm, you're wet," he moaned in between kisses. I nodded and arched my back in pleasure. "Kieran, I don't want to wait," he said, looking up at me.

I nodded quickly and he moved up to kiss me.

"Are you sure?" he asked.

I nodded.

He nodded too and kissed me deeply. He gently placed himself between my legs and started to rub there soaking up the moisture, then gently began to push. I grimaced from the expectation of pain. My heartbeat quickened and I could feel myself sweating all over. He pushed a little harder.

"No, stop," I said quickly.

"Does it hurt?" he asked. It hadn't even begun to hurt. It wasn't far enough, or in at all, to hurt. I was just freaked out about it and shook my head. "It's okay, it's fine," he said quietly and kissed me. "We can try again some other time."

But it did no good. We semi-tried over the next two weeks but each time he got close, I backed off and freaked out and said no. He never pressured me about it. He was always understanding, though I didn't quite understand myself. I wanted to make love to him. I was ready and yet every time we tried, I had to stop. I wondered if there was something wrong with me but pushed the thought out of my mind. I wanted us to enjoy our holiday. I didn't want it focused around one thing which may or may not happen. Of course we had the perfect surroundings; no parents to worry about, no relatives that may spot us on our evening stroll, no worries or pressures but I still couldn't let myself go. I still couldn't give in to him. I scolded myself about it. I mean, you hear about twelve-year-olds getting pregnant and here we were, two fully grown adults and we couldn't manage what is meant to be the most natural thing on earth. I tried not to worry about it and concentrated on pleasing him in other ways. See, that's another confusing thing. It wasn't some deep-rooted fear that I was going against my religion. It wasn't something inherent that was so ingrained in me that I couldn't do it. We did everything else, all of it which was so wrong but I just couldn't go all the way. Despite my frustrations with it, we had a good time.

On the fifth day of our holiday, Zahid and I had a minor tiff about something inconsequential. I locked myself in the bathroom and began to cry. I heard a knock on the door.

"Kieran, are you okay?" I heard him say.

I said nothing but sobbed to myself.

He knocked again. "Kieran, are you crying? Please open the door."

"No," I said through my tears.

"What's wrong?" he asked, obviously concerned at how upset I sounded. I could not answer because I did not really know myself. The argument we had had was nothing serious and certainly no worse than the hundreds of other arguments we had had before. I was taking the pill because I did not want to have my period on holiday. Perhaps it was making me feel a little unbalanced. Zahid continued to plead with me to open the door. I sat there crying until my eyes were red raw and I had a headache. My shoulders sagged and I finally opened the door.

Zahid took one look at me and scooped me into his arms. "Kieran, I'm sorry. I didn't mean any of it. I didn't mean to upset you so much."

"No," I said into his shoulder. "It's not you."

"Then what is it? Are you missing your family?"

I looked up at him and shook my head.

"What is it?"

"I don't know."

"You don't know?"

I shook my head.

"You crazy girl, come here." He kissed my forehead, held me tight and didn't question me any further.

The truth is I still don't know why I cried so much that day. It wasn't the first or last time I had done it. Sometimes I cried for no reason at all. I just felt sad and locked myself up and cried for a long time. I don't know whether it was some stupid psychological thing that no doubt could only be resolved through hours of therapy or if it was me just letting off steam. Sometimes people needed to cry. I left it at that.

The rest of the holiday was a real success. We had good food and good times and left Tunisia browner than when we landed and happy. Really happy.

I crept into the house quietly. I had put on my long black coat to hide my black figure-hugging slash-neck top and faded blue Levis. I wore Western clothes to university but always covered up with a coat as I felt uncomfortable parading around in front of my parents with trousers on. I tiptoed up the stairs, trying my best not to wake anyone. They all knew I had been on holiday but seeing me enter the house with a suitcase would make it all too real for my parents. To see me walk down the stairs in my pyjamas would allow them to forget easier where I had been. Well, that was my theory anyway.

I changed and unpacked to the sounds of the house stirring and awaking. I called Zahid to see how he was doing. It was pathetic but I missed him already. He didn't pick up but I smiled anyway and breathed a sigh of contentment. It was weird because even though I did my best to push him away sometimes, this holiday had really bought us closer. Sometimes I found it so weird that he was this whole other person entirely separate from me yet I felt like he knew me so well and was a part of me. It all sounds so clichéd but that's the only way I can explain it. It's like you spend so much time with someone and you get used to them being there and then you realise that they are this different and separate being that you may never have met if your lives had taken a different path. Well, anyway, enough of the philosophy, it was time to face the family.

I padded down the stairs, bracing myself. I knew they wouldn't say anything. After all, they had allowed me to go. It's just that it felt so awkward. I entered the kitchen and my parents turned.

"When did you get back?" asked my mother.

"Early this morning," I replied.

"Good flight? You eat properly?" asked my dad.

I nodded.

"Good," he replied.

"How did you get home?" asked my mother.

"Train."

"What about the other girls?"

"Train as well."

She made a low grunting noise but said nothing further. I grabbed some juice and went back upstairs. *Okay, so that was relatively painless,* I thought and walked up to my room.

"Damn," I said under my breath. I had left my keys downstairs. I ran down to retrieve them when I heard my parents talking in hushed tones. I crept closer to the kitchen straining to block out Sania's *'Nahin Jeena'* blasting from her stereo.

"It's time," my father was saying. "Of course they will say they have to study but they can study when we come back."

Come back? I thought. *Come back from where?*

"All three of them will go," he said.

"Go where?" I asked, entering the kitchen as nonchalantly as I could.

My father turned sharply in my direction. I looked at him questioningly.

He stayed silent for a moment and then said, "Bangladesh."

The name struck me with such force that I physically stepped back. "Bangladesh? Who? When?"

"We are all going this summer in two weeks' time," he said. "For two months."

"Two months?" I said. "All of us?" I felt a quiet panic rising in my chest. "I can't go this summer."

"What do you mean you can't go?" asked my mother. "We are all going."

"But I can't. I have my final year coming up. I need this summer to get organised."

"You can bring your books," said my father.

"It's not about taking books. I have a final year project coming up. I need to stay in touch with my tutors, sort a project out, do research. I need a computer and - "

"I'll buy you a computer there," said my father, cutting me short.

"No," I tried desperately. "I need the Internet. I can't leave."

"But you went on holiday," said my mum.

"For two weeks!" I said, trying to keep control of my voice. "How is two weeks the same thing as two months? I'm not going. I can't."

"You are going," said my father. "And that's final."

"You don't understand," I persisted. "My whole degree will go down the drain if I go. Everything I have worked for is for this project that I have to do. If I mess it up, then everything is messed up."

"There is more to life than study," my mother interjected.

"You're a smart girl," said my father. "You will catch up."

"It's not about catching up!" I yelled. "I can't go."

"Well, who is going to look after you, eh?" yelled my father. "Who will cook for you and feed you? What are you going to do on your own!?"

"I can look after myself," I said.

"You can't even cook," chimed in my mother.

"I can learn!" I yelled back.

"Just be quiet." My father turned away from me.

"I'm not going," I said and walked out with red cheeks and blazing eyes. How could they just go ahead and book tickets without asking us? I knew what this was about. Of course I knew. This was about getting Shelly and me and maybe even Neha married off. A batch deal. I'd heard about it happening to other girls but I never thought my parents would try to pull a stunt like that. I was so angry. All I knew was that I wasn't going. My dad was powerful, firm and strong but where it counted, I was stronger. I had resolve, endless unwavering resolve and when I put my mind to something, God help the person who tried to change it. I paced my room angrily.

Marriage, or at least arranged marriage, was about finding someone that your daughter/son was compatible with; someone you could see them building a life with. It was a process that should be carried out carefully with your full concentration and focus.

How could they do that when there was a queue of three? How could they focus on us individually when trying to find three husbands in the space of two months? Who can be discerning when they're in a race against time? I sat on my bed in anger. Neha was still asleep and Shelly was in Manchester. She had spent a lot of time there as part of her new job. This was a cause for concern for my parents and a source of much gossip and disdain with our neighbours. You could almost hear them whispering *"Istigfarullah! How could they let their daughter go and stay alone in another city?"* It was 10 a.m. which meant that Shelly was most likely to be asleep too.

I called Rayya and explained the situation to her but she didn't give me the support I expected.

"Can't you even go for two weeks?" she asked. "You *do* get four months off."

I grimaced. I didn't want my parents to know that I got four months off university but knowing Rayya, she would tell them. "I can't," I insisted to her. "This year is the most important year of university. It's probably the most important year of my life! It's going to decide the class of my degree. Afa, I can't just leave everything and go," I pleaded.

"I don't know," she replied. "You can't stay here on your own."

"I won't be!" I yelled. "You're here. Jasmine is here."

"Yeah, but we won't be living with you," she said. I drooped. I didn't actually have a right to hassle her about this. There were much bigger things going on in her life. Her husband had been diagnosed with colon cancer a few weeks before and they were going through some tough times. She was under a lot of pressure and I felt that my problem was nothing compared to what she was going through. It's funny how I've always been the kind of person that believes that bad stuff just won't happen to them. Even though my own father has survived two heart attacks and now my brother-in-law had cancer, I still felt like things like that would never happen to me. Perhaps it was because I felt that fate had dealt me a hard blow in life anyway, it couldn't get crueller. But you never know. You just never know.

As soon as Neha woke up, I told her about their plan. I was surprised to see that both she and Sania were really excited by the prospect. "Don't you understand? They're planning to get us married off," I said.

"All three of you?" Sania laughed. "No, Dad said we're gonna go to get Shelly married."

I shook my head at them but they simply continued chattering away about what they were going to buy for the trip and what they were going to do.

The phone rang once, twice, three times before he picked up.

"Hello," he said cheerily.

"Zahid?"

"Yeah?"

"It's me," I said quietly.

"Everything go okay at home?"

"Yeah," I said softly.

"What's wrong?" he asked, immediately picking up that I wasn't normal. I told him everything in one breath. He was silent for a few seconds.

"Zahid?"

"I'm just thinking," he replied.

"Thinking what?"

"They're gonna try and get you married, right?"

"Yeah."

"Don't go."

"Well it's not as easy as that, is it?"

"You *can't* go."

"Zahid, don't you get it? It's not as easy as that," I repeated, slightly irritated.

"Kieran, look, I gotta drop my sister off. I'll call you back later, ok?" he said and rushed off.

I stared at the phone in disbelief. What the hell was wrong with him? I needed some reassurance, some support but he was too goddamned busy for me. I was pissed off and slammed the phone against the receiver. At times like this, I felt so lonely and so helpless.

Oh, Jesus, you know what? I'm gonna stop. I'm gonna stop being this moany cow who's always going on about the bad things in her life. At the end of the day, I have a roof over my head and food to eat and there are worse places to be in life, right? I haven't had it rosy but if someone I knew was always moaning like this, I would be getting pissed off right about now at how negative they were. The thing is, half of me really isn't like this. Half of me is great and funny and silly and kooky and cool. Half of me is happy. I refuse to wear a watch, I hate jewellery, I am unbeatable at Connect4, I know the words to 'Notorious Thugz', I would never dye my hair, I would never read 'Lord of the Flies' again. Those are the things that make me, me. Not my family and not my boyfriend. Yes, all the trials in my life have shaped who I am and yes, they are a part of me and I need to talk about them but it doesn't mean I can't talk about anything else, right?

Rayya came round later that week and took our passports so that her husband could put visas on them. I tried to explain my situation to her. I told her that I could not afford to go because of my studies but she simply said that that is what our dad and her husband wanted. I wanted to yell at her and ask her why our lives and actions were always subject to the whims of men.

I told them in clear terms that if I went, I would only stay for two weeks and no more, which of course didn't faze them. I told them time and again that I would not get married because I wanted to finish my studies first. They all nodded in what I knew was mock agreement. I was so angry and helpless. I kept reiterating the question of how they expected to find someone for me to marry in two weeks. "We're not planning for you to get married," they insisted, blatantly lying to me. "I don't want to go," I replied back each time.

This went on for a week until finally my father surrendered. I was delighted at the news. I think he finally realised that I was completely serious about not wanting to get married and he knew it would be a waste of time and money if I went for a mere two weeks. I knew that my sisters would keep tabs on me, in fact Rayya was going to come and stay for two weeks and Jasmine for one week but the prospect of two whole months without the constant stress and noise of my family filled me with such a sense of happiness that I couldn't wait until they left.

Their day of departure finally arrived and I woke up that morning with a sense of contentment. I had taken on an extra shift at work because I did not want to get caught up in their last-minute rush and arguments, and had said my goodbyes the night before. I still could not believe that my dad had given in and agreed to leave me here. I walked downstairs past the huge suitcases in the corridors. I felt no sadness. I knew I wasn't going to miss them. I know that sounds horrible but when you've lived nineteen years of your life with a crazy family like mine, any time alone is precious. I wasn't planning on throwing a house party or going out clubbing or any of the things a normal person would do in my situation. I just wanted some peace and quiet; some time to think, time where I wouldn't be questioned about every little thing, time to watch what *I* wanted to watch. I opened the door. "Bismillah Ir Rahman Ir Rahim," I said under my breath and stepped out with a huge smile on my face.

Jasmine stayed for the first few days which was fine but I couldn't wait to get the place to myself. When I did, neighbours came knocking almost every day for the first week. I always said that my elder sister was staying with me. An unmarried girl staying at home alone (even if it is her family home) was definitely going to incite endless gossip and criticism. Rayya called me every day at 6.30 p.m. I think she figured that by then I would have finished any overtime I was doing at work and definitely be at home. It grated on my nerves a little but I suppose that's the trade-off for being allowed to live alone for two months.

"No, trust me. It's all about the postcode."

"Oh shut up, it isn't!" said Ashley as she threw a handful of grass at Zain.

"It *is,"* he insisted. "Watch; you two are gonna do well in your lives because you live in posh areas and went to posh schools."

"But if you're intelligent, you will do well regardless of where you studied," countered James.

"Yes, but the postcode still comes into play. If you and I went for a job interview, if we had got exactly the same grades all throughout our lives, *you* would get the job coz of where you studied," said Zain firmly.

"No, no, no, that's not true," replied Ashley. "It's how well you do in the interview."

"Yes, but if we'd done equally well and they couldn't decide, that would be the deciding factor."

"Just coz you went to a shit school," said James.

"Hey!" said Zain. "I'm proud of where I came from. I'm proud of not coming from an all-boys grammar school for toffs."

"It was mixed!" insisted James.

"Besides, it's way cooler being common," said Zain.

"Not when you're going on about how cool you are. People who insist they're cool are not cool," said James.

"So who's for ice cream?" I interrupted before the conversation could reach a new low. I gestured towards the ice cream van that was parked at the edge of the green. Ashley nodded and James and Zain briefly stopped their debate to tell me what flavour they wanted. I wandered off towards the van.

This is the life, I thought. Lazy Saturday evenings in the park with friends; no parents to grill me about where I was going, who I was going with, what time I would be back. I could get used to this life. I bought three chocolate and one strawberry ice cream and walked back towards my friends who were strewn about on the Surrey Quays lawn. I handed out the ice creams and settled back down onto the grass.

"In some ways, I wish she would," James was saying.

"Who would do what?" I asked, taking a bite out of my ice cream.

"I was just talking about how my mum's left me to my own devices marriage-wise. But I wish she would actually get a wife for me," he said.

"Why?" I said. "Trust me, it's much better that you're allowed to choose."

"I know, but where the hell am I supposed to find a nice woman? It would be easier if my mum sorted it out for me," he insisted.

I just shook my head.

"What about you, Zain?" asked Ashley, "Your parents looking to get you hitched any time soon?"

"Nah, they're letting me work for a few years. Get some money together," he said.

"Yeah, it's okay for guys. They can wait until they're about twenty seven or so but girls… at twenty four, they're 'over the hill'," I said with mild annoyance.

Ashley sighed and commented on how lucky she was she didn't have to go through all of that. I nodded in agreement and returned to my ice cream.

The weather was gorgeous. The balmy evening had the perfect mixture of warm air and a cool breeze. We lazed there until late into the evening. I thought how wonderful this was - to be able to enjoy an evening in the company of my friends, just chilling out. I had never been a materialistic girl. When one's possessions are under constant threat of being stolen, one learns not to be materialistic. This is what I really enjoyed: good conversation with people that I liked. I had told Rayya that I would be going out with friends and that I would be back before nine. It was 8.30 p.m. No doubt she had called the house a few times already. I checked my phone but there were no messages, which was good. I walked home in quiet contentment. I was happy.

The next morning was Sunday. I stretched lazily in my bed and yawned. It had been two weeks since my family had gone and I didn't miss them at all. I loved having my own space and time. I made myself a light breakfast and flicked through a pile of magazines that Shelly had left me. "Asian Woman," I said, grabbing a magazine from the middle of the pile. I scanned the cover with mild interest and flicked through the magazine.

There were pages and pages of advertisements which were probably more interesting than the features. Gorgeous models in gorgeous outfits adorned every other page. I shook my head at how beautiful some of them were. I knew that with the right make-up and lighting, most young Asian girls could look beautiful but these women were stunning. I silently thanked God that most of these women existed in the perfect pages of beauty magazines and not walking the streets of everyday life. Girls on the street were practically clones of each other: dyed brown hair, coloured contact lenses, high heels, low-cut tops with tiny handbags in one hand and mobile phones in the other. I did my best to avoid all of that... Well, apart from the heels. We all need a bit of height in our lives!

I lazed around for the rest of the day. While I was moisturising myself after a bath, the phone began to ring.

"Two guesses who that's gonna be," I muttered to myself and rushed to get the phone.

"Hello?" I answered breathlessly.

"Hello?" asked a familiar voice.

"Hello?" I repeated.

"It's Zahid."

"Zahid! What are you doing calling my house?"

"Well, no one else is home," he said sheepishly.

"I know but that's not the point. What if someone *was* home?" I asked.

"I got a favour to ask," he said.

"What?"

"Can I come round?" he asked cheekily.

"What? No way. NO WAY."

"Oh, come on Kieran. I'm horny."

"No Zahid. There's no way."

"Oh, come on. There's no one there. I could sneak in and sneak out before anyone sees me."

I did really want to see him. Between sorting out a final year project and his family commitments this summer, he had hardly any time for me. Regardless of this, I couldn't risk him being seen.

"Kieran, please. I swear, I'll be so discreet. No one will ever know." He spent a few more minutes convincing me before I finally relented.

"Zahid, if someone sees you, I am personally going to castrate you, ok?" I said.

"Deal. I'll be there in half an hour," he said.

"Call me when you get here. Call me at the end of my street. We have to be really careful, Zahid, okay? I know it's dark but knowing this street, there's *always* someone looking out of their window."

"No one will know I'm there," he said.

I spent the next half an hour in a flurry between making myself beautiful and trying to calm myself down. If someone saw him, that really would be the end of me. I couldn't believe I had given into him. Only stupid teenagers in movies thought they could pull off a stunt like this! I drank some Coke to calm myself down which of course, only served to do the opposite. Zahid and I had been through 'movie scene' situations before, where we were caught in the disabled toilets at university, making out like a pair of sex-crazed adolescents but this was much more serious.

I pretended to put the rubbish out and subtly opened our gate so it would be open for when Zahid slipped into the house. I took a furtive glance up and down the street to make sure that no one was around. As I closed the door, my mobile rang.

"Where are you?" I asked.

"At the top of your street."

"Is there anyone around?"

"No."

"What number are you at?"

"Eighteen."

"Okay, I will open my door, come straight in and for God's sake do it quickly."

"Okay."

I opened the door and prayed that the same thing would not happen next door. Zahid appeared at the gate and quickly walked in. I shut and locked the door and tried to calm my thumping heart. "Did anyone see you?" I asked quickly.

"No."

"Are you sure?"

"Yes." A smile crept across his face.

"What?"

"You look nice," he said reaching for me.

I slapped his hand away. "You're such a pervert!"

"Oi! I didn't come here for your scintillating conversational skills." He reached for me again. This time I let him wrap his arms around me. His hands slid down my back and he pressed me against him. I instantly felt his hard-on.

"Jeez, you don't waste any time," I said. "Come on, let's go upstairs." I felt awkward standing in my living room with him. He didn't resist so I quickly lead him up the stairs. I shut my bedroom door and turned to face him.

"I missed you," he said, grabbing my arms and drawing me to him. He kissed me for a long time. He lifted the slip I was wearing and slid his hands under. He slid his hands over my stomach up to my breasts and started to caress them softly as he kissed me hard. He lifted the slip over my head and dropped it onto the floor. He then stepped out of his shoes and unzipped his trousers. He hooked his fingers into the elastic of my knickers and pulled them down. They dropped to the floor and I stood naked before him. I undressed him and we became more frenzied in our actions. I looked up at him.

"Zahid, I want to try," I said.

He shook his head. "I don't want tonight to be about trying. I just want to enjoy you." I understood where he was coming from. In Tunisia, we had tried and failed and it was disheartening. He was right; if we concentrated only on having sex, the night could be ruined. I nodded and kissed him deeply. There were plenty of ways to have fun without penetration. After about two hours, we lay in an exhausted heap. He traced small circles around one of my breasts. He looked into my eyes.

"You're mine," he said with a smile. I nodded and kissed him. I wished we could lie like that all night but I knew that he had to get back. Eventually, we got up, showered and dressed. He left me after a series of long kisses. I was really happy. It was sickening but I was really in love with him. We did the whole 007 routine in order to get him out of the house unseen and I closed the door with a smile. It was times like this that I knew I had to be with him regardless of what my parents would say or do. *All in good time,* I thought. All in good time.

Chapter 6. Changes

"Damnit!" I yelled as I rushed out of the bathroom with the towel wrapped around me haphazardly. The phone had rang about four times in the past half hour during which I was in the shower, each call going on for about twenty rings. No doubt it was Rayya.

"Hello?" I said without disguising my annoyance.

"Kieran?" said Rayya.

I rolled my eyes. "Yeah?"

"I called loads of times. Where were you?"

"I was in the shower. I heard the phone going on."

"Oh, right. What have you been up to?"

"Nothing," I said, slightly nervous that someone had seen Zahid yesterday. "How is *dula-bhai?*" I asked after my brother-in-law.

"He's okay; in pain which is to be expected. He's finished his chemotherapy. They're starting him on radiotherapy soon."

"And when is the operation set for?"

"A few weeks after mum and them come back."

"Kids okay?"

"Yeah, kids are fine. So listen, are you ready for the news?"

"What news?"

"They've found husbands for Shelly and Neha."

"What?" I was completely knocked for six.

"Yep. Remember how I said they had shown Neha that guy from Gonargow that she liked and they were waiting for Shelly?"

"Yeah… "

"Well, they found Shelly one now."

"What? Who? I can't believe they managed it so quickly!" They were only two weeks into their two-month trip.

"Shahin," she said simply.

I missed a beat. "What?"

"Shahin," she repeated.

"You gotta be kidding me."

"Nope."

"What do you mean 'Shahin'? Shahin as in *Shahin?*" I asked incredulously.

"Yeah."

"What's going on? What… " I struggled for words.

"Apparently they've been bugging her about him for two weeks and she just agreed."

"What do you mean 'she just agreed'? Did they do something to her? Are they forcing her?"

"No. I spoke to Neha and she said that they've been texting each other and Shelly looks really happy."

"How could she agree?" I asked, shaking my head in disbelief.

Shahin was my dad's nephew so basically, our first cousin. He was about forty years old and his mother had been trying to get one of my sisters (Rayya, then Jasmine and now Shelly) to marry him for the past ten years. He seemed like a complete creep. But regardless of that, there was the fact that he was a *first cousin*. See, that's another thing I may as well address. In our culture, it is deemed okay for first cousins to marry each other. I just couldn't understand how they couldn't see that it was completely wrong. I had a bunch of nieces and nephews, and to think that they would marry each other when they were older was crazy. And the medical implications were also extremely serious. I just don't think people understood how wrong it was. Now, I'm not saying that all Bengali or Pakistani people are like this but I heard too much of it to think that it didn't happen. It happened all the time. It was happening to my own sister.

"How could she agree?" I asked again. "I mean, he seems like such a perve!"

"I don't know. I'm in shock too. It hasn't really sunk in yet."

"Have you talked to her? Is she thinking straight?"

"No, I don't know."

"Have you told Jasmine?"

"Yeah, I told her. She was so pissed off. She's sure that they're pressuring her."

"But I told her before she went not to let anyone pressure her. I know what she's like so I made sure I spoke to her and told her not to say yes to a guy she wasn't happy with. What is she thinking?"

"That's the thing though. Neha and Sania say that she's really happy. He buys her things, they spend a lot of time together and apparently they flirt all the time."

"Oh God, I really don't wanna hear it!" I shook my head.

"I don't know, Kieran. I spoke to Mum but she said the same thing, that everyone is really happy."

"I don't know what to say."

"I know exactly what you mean."

"What about Neha's guy? Is he okay?"

"Yeah, everyone really likes him. The date is set one week after Shelly's wedding."

"So when is Shelly's wedding?"

"End of the week."

"The end of *this* week?" I exclaimed.

"Yes. This week, Sunday."

"God." We were both silent for a minute and then because we didn't know what else to say, said our goodbyes and hung up.

I busied myself with cooking pasta and rolled the thought of my sisters getting married around in my head. It was a big deal but somehow, I wasn't all geared up for it. I just couldn't believe they had sorted it out so quickly. I had doubted that my parents would be organised enough to sort out one marriage let alone two. I couldn't believe it was really going to happen. It was just too weird. I decided not to think about it and went upstairs to enjoy my pasta over the evening's edition of 'CSI'.

Later on that week, I met Jasmine for lunch. She worked at the Bank of England as an Administrative Assistant. I knew she was dissatisfied with her work because she deeply regretted not going to university, however, she put up with it because it was a job and generated income. I met her at Exit 2 of Bank station and turned left towards the bank. Jasmine was wearing a pair of pinstripe black trousers and a beige twin set. I smoothed down my knee-length tweed coat and hoped I looked okay. I knew the bank was full of all these posh types so I didn't want to look like a complete scrub.

We walked through the grand entrance hall and a security guard scanned my bag with a metal detector. I smiled my thanks and followed Jasmine through a set of corridors.

"I work on the second floor," she said, pushing a button in the lift. "I'll show you my office. You can leave your coat up there if you want." We walked into her open-plan office and she showed me her desk proudly.

"Looking good," I remarked, taking stock of the spacious office. On our way to the dinner hall, we passed a tall white man dressed in neatly pressed black trousers and a blue shirt. He had light blonde hair and smiled as he held the door open for Jasmine and I.

"This is one of my managers," said Jasmine as we passed him. I felt awkward as we had not been introduced properly so I just smiled hello and goodbye as we walked on. *He'll probably just put it down to the bad etiquette of Asians,* I thought.

As we walked downstairs, I mentally noted the number of men who held doors open for us. It was such a simple and gentlemanly thing to do but I had hardly come across it before. Of course, there were men who had held doors open for me in the past but growing up in a predominantly Asian area, I had hardly come across this brand of mild-mannered English gentleman. Asian boys on the street were more likely to shout "Alright Princess?" than hold a door open for a woman. I felt silly at how touched I was by this simple gesture.

"Usually this place is full of suits but luckily it's Friday so a lot of departments have dressed down," said Jasmine as we set down our plates on a cafeteria table.

"These 'suits' you speak of seem alright, actually. The number of men that held doors open for us… "

"Oh, they're all like that. They're just so different. People here are like from a whole different world to us."

"Your manager seems nice."

"Alistair? He is. I didn't really like him at first but he's grown on me."

"Why didn't you like him?"

"Actually, it's something silly. He's like a proper posh educated guy right? He's originally from New Zealand and when he first met me, he asked me if I was a 'bona fide East Ender'. I said yes and he seemed so proud of the fact that he knew of us. Like, he was so worldly because he had met someone common like me. He's probably really happy that he met you too coz now he can talk about how he met *two* 'lowly' people."

I smiled and thought that we could never be like them. I suppose it's true what they say: good breeding always shows. We finished lunch. I said goodbye and left.

The next day flew by and Sunday arrived. I didn't really feel anything. I wasn't going to be at the wedding, obviously, and Shelly was getting married to some creep I severely disliked. I didn't know what the hell was going on but it was happening and there was nothing I could do about it… story of my life. It's strange because when you're young, you convince yourself that you are in control of your destiny; that you always have control over a situation. I've always believed that I was the kind of person who would *act* in a situation I was not comfortable in; act to make it better or act to get myself out of the situation. I saw myself as a determined, focused, driven individual who was going to achieve her ambitions and get what she wanted out of life. But it was always tomorrow or next week or next year. I hated living at home and yet I continued to do so. I comforted myself by looking at it as *when* I get out, not *if*. I was finishing my degree next year and then life would begin. Then I would be free.

As expected, the week after Shelly's wedding flew by and Neha was also wedded. I didn't know how to feel about her wedding either. I had never met the man she was marrying; indeed, neither had she until two weeks before her wedding. A few days after Neha's wedding, Rayya called me. She told me that Shelly and Neha were both happy. She said that Neha's in-laws were very religious and they had her wearing the full *hijab* in the summer heat. I felt sorry for her discomfort but knew that it was nothing compared to what she would face later in life. Due to her hearing impairment, she had great difficulty communicating with people. A husband who could not read, write or speak English was not going to help her at all. My parents simply did not consider things like that. They came from the gutter and they were fully content to stay there. I don't want to sound like a snob but shouldn't parents want better for their children? Someone who can provide them with a better life? It seemed as though my parents didn't care who we got married to just as long as we got married; just as long as people couldn't whisper about us and shake their heads in disapproval.

Before long, it was time for my family to return. I had known that I wouldn't miss them during their time away but I thought perhaps I would begin to feel lonely, however, that wasn't the case. I woke up that day with a heavy heart. Even though I had thoroughly enjoyed my two months without them, I felt like I hadn't done enough; hadn't seen my friends enough. Zahid had been so busy, he had hardly spent any time with me.

I glanced at the clock as it neared 8 p.m.; their estimated time of arrival. At 8.30 p.m., the small people-carrier parked outside our house. I walked out to greet them and help with the baggage. When I saw them, I gave my sisters and my father long hugs and my mother a brief, awkward one. Immediately, the house descended into the chaos it was so used to. My pristine kitchen was in a mess before I could even say "Mr Muscle" and the tidy living room became a base for the endless array of suitcases hauled out of the van. My sisters and I lugged the suitcases in one-by-one. We were used to doing this type of thing since my dad was too old and my brothers were no good for anything. When we painted the house, it was my sisters and I who did it. When we had our house re-carpeted, it was my sisters and I who moved the furniture from one room to another. When we bought a new set of beds, my sisters and I took them up the long winding stairs and set them up. We did the 'women's work' as well as the 'men's work'.

The month after my family came back, I heard my parents whispering in hushed tones, which was never a good sign.

I walked in breezily. *"Kita oyser?"* I asked them what had happened.

My mother said nothing and my father simply sipped his tea.

I said nothing until finally my mother said, "Your brother's in jail."

I felt a burst of joy. Finally, that bastard had got his come-uppance. "What happened? They catch him buying drugs or something?"

My parents both looked at me. "No, not Kamal - Javed," said my mother.

I felt my joy deflate. They were talking about my older brother. Well, if you can call him my brother. I saw him about twice a year and knew hardly anything about his life. He had made a Hindu girl pregnant and, despite my parents pleading with him to leave her and marry a Muslim girl, he had stuck by her. I guess it is admirable that he chose to stay with her and support his child but to my parent's dismay, he had not only stood by her, but proceeded to have three more children with her out of wedlock. This was 'disgraceful' on many levels. It was wrong to consort with Hindu people 'in that way'. Muslims can only marry Muslims and that was one of the most fundamental laws of our religion. And to have four children out of wedlock was unheard of. My parents would have been a bit more accepting if she had chosen to convert to Islam but she hadn't. I had never met her and had only seen the eldest two of his children when he had bought them round to our house a while back.

"What has he done this time?" I asked, unfazed by their revelation.

They looked at me disapprovingly. "We don't know," replied my mother.

I shrugged. "God knows what will become of his children," I remarked.

"Well, that's the thing," said my mother "She's in jail too."

"Who?" I asked.

"The Hindu cow. She's in prison too."

I looked at my mother in shock. "What do you mean she's in prison too?"

"They tried to steal a TV or something from where Javed works and they got caught."

"What do you mean 'they'? What did *she* do?"

"I don't know but she was there too so they're both in prison right now."

"Where are the kids?"

"With one of their neighbours. I talked to her this morning, some Punjabi woman."

"What's going to happen to them?"

My parents were silent so I repeated my question.

"They're coming to stay," said my mother.

"What?"

"Well, what else?" she said.

I didn't know what to think. I knew they were my niece and nephews but I had hardly seen them. It wasn't like my parents had disowned my brother (he was male after all) but he had just chosen to stay away from our house. I didn't blame him. If I had a chance to start my own life and never come home, I would do so too. I knew it wasn't the children's fault but I couldn't help but think selfishly. It was my last year at university and I was struggling with a final year project. The last thing I needed was four children running about the house. I mean, if it was Rayya's kids then fair enough because I saw them as my own. I loved them and would do anything for them. These kids, however, were like total strangers. No, they *were* total strangers.

"How long are they staying for?" I asked.

"Well, he's in for eighteen months and she's in for twelve months," said my mother.

"What!?" I asked incredulously. "The kids are going to be staying with us for a year!?"

"Ask your father," said my mother and walked out.

I turned to my dad. His face was worn but stern. "What else can we do? They're our flesh and blood," he said.

"I understand that, but can't they go somewhere else? Doesn't she have any relatives?" I asked.

"*Hindu* relatives?" He shook his head. "These children need some faith in their lives. They don't know what they are. They're not Muslim and they're not Hindu. This is our chance to instil something good in them."

"But how on earth are you going to afford it? It's not like *Bhaisaab* has any savings!"

"You're just like your mother," my dad retorted. His words stung and I said nothing. "They have nowhere else to go," he finished.

And so they descended on our house. I know I sound completely heartless but it made the house even more unbearable than it already was. I tried to be affectionate towards them but found there was no real feeling there. His children were like animals. I know that sounds terrible but it's true. They were uncultured, dirty, messy and noisy. I couldn't believe their behaviour. They simply did not listen to requests and instructions and behaved like savages. They also ate as if they were never fed. I don't know how their mother treated them but at every meal, these children ate twice as much as I, an adult, could manage. It was terrible and sad.

I remember one day walking past the toilet and Javed's middle son was pulling up his trousers. He didn't use tissue or water to cleanse himself.

He simply pulled up his trousers. I couldn't believe it. Muslims must use water to cleanse themselves after using the toilet and doing something like this was abhorrent. I shook my head at their upbringing. Muslim or not, these children had had no basic guidance in any aspect of their lives.

I felt thankful that I had been bought up with religion. It instils a sense of respect for a higher power. It didn't really matter whether that religion was Islam or Hinduism or Christianity or anything else. Believing in God does something for the soul and the mind. I'm not saying that the Atheists and Agnostics of the world are savages. I'm just saying that I personally believe that having something to believe in does a lot of good for a person.

My mother tried to teach Javed's children the *Kalimas* and about the five pillars of Islam, the cornerstones of our faith. The kids didn't know what the hell they were doing. I knew it was terrible for them to have their parents ripped away from them like this but still I could not muster love for them, only pity. It's all good and well saying, "At the end of the day, they are our flesh and blood and we are responsible for them," but the day-to-day logistics of it was a nightmare. My mother had already raised eight children, albeit not too successfully, and to be thrown into caring for four young children made her crankier than she had been for a long time. There were meals to prepare, nappies to change and fights to resolve. Bathing, clothing, feeding and changing the children took the energy out of everyone. The house had this constant tense atmosphere. Even my father began to question his good intentions. He was getting no welfare money for the children and the financial and emotional strain was proving to be too much. He was sixty-six years old, an age for peace and reflection. Instead, he woke up amid screams and shouts and endless whining.

Their mother had the gall to tell my father that the children couldn't change school and therefore he had to wake up at seven-thirty every morning and take them all the way to St. John's Wood. I couldn't believe it when I heard that. I told my dad, No, let the social workers sort this one out. My dad was too old to be trekking around with three kids in tow.

The worst thing about it all was that my parents didn't question my brother about what he had done to end up in prison. He offered no explanation, no financial assistance and no apologies. My parents unquestioningly supported him, which of course is what parents are meant to do for their children. It's a pity they forgot that daughters count as children as well.

Neha felt the strain of it more than me. She was away from her husband, thinking about how to get him over to this country, struggling at university and now had to spend every spare minute looking after the children. I felt like the house would implode but as always, there was nothing we could do. My brothers got into trouble and my parents bailed them out. It was the circle of life.

It wasn't long before my father started to scout for a husband for me. I avoided the issue as much as possible. I didn't want to think about it, at least until after I had finished my degree. The first guy they came up with had twelve brothers and sisters. I balked at the figure when Rayya first told me.

"TWELVE brothers and sisters," I exclaimed.

"Yeah, but don't worry, they're all grown up so you won't have to look after any of them."

"Yeah, but *twelve,*" I said incredulously. "What type of people have twelve bloody children?"

"What do you mean by that?"

"Well," I tried to find the right words. "Would you have married someone with twelve brothers and sisters?"

"Why not?"

I looked at her disbelievingly. "Because it's… How can someone have twelve children? I mean, don't they have any sense of planning or organisation or hope for their children's futures?"

"Well, what about us? There are eight of us."

"Oh, and look how brilliantly we all turned out!" I almost yelled. "And four extra children make a lot of difference, Afa. There's no way I'm marrying someone with twelve brothers and sisters. That's just ridiculous."

My sisters couldn't understand why I thought it was so wrong. Luckily, Jasmine was on my side and insisted that twelve brothers and sisters equalled more family to meet/greet and inevitably have arguments with because that's what happens in Asian families. In-laws just bitch and bitch and bitch about each other. They tried to persuade me to at least meet him but I said a straight no. I couldn't understand why they thought it was so normal. I mean, yes, Asian people do tend to have large families but twelve children was bordering on ridiculous. How can you possibly give twelve children the time, energy and resources they need to grow into well-developed and balanced individuals? I could see my sisters' point in that we also grew up without any guidance and most of us turned out okay but 'most' just wasn't good enough.

I threw myself into my studies. Zahid and I helped each other through our final year projects. It was a tough slog and at times I despaired because there was so much work to do. I stayed up into the early hours of the morning, programming away thoughtlessly. I thought the bulk of my work would be completed by December but January came and I still hadn't done even fifty percent of what needed to be done. We worked like dogs through January and by February, we were a little more relaxed.

We had been together for a year and a half now and he had become a part of me. I still found it weird that he was this whole other person, someone totally separate from me who I hadn't known for eighteen years of my life. I couldn't imagine being without him. Sometimes I worried about the future. What would happen when Dad found me another prospective suitor? What was I going to do about Zahid? There was no way on earth I could tell my family about him because they would simply kill me. Zahid was a good man and a good Muslim and that's all that should matter but of course, because he was *Pakistani* and not *Bengali*, it was impossible. We talked about it often and he always said, "Let's cross that bridge when we come to it," which seemed like a cop-out to me. My parents were still actively searching and Zahid and I had to make some decisions. I knew at crunch time, I would give in to my parents because I respected my father too much to tell him that I wanted to marry a Pakistani man. I knew it would break my heart but I didn't have the courage to stand against my parent's wishes. I just hoped they could find someone decent. The disgrace of having a drug-addict brother and another brother in prison was enough to scare anyone away.

Javed's four children had been with us for four months when we heard some good news. Sasha, Javed's girlfriend, was being released early. Apparently, she had won the appeal and was given compassion for the fact that she was a mother of four. I nearly fainted with joy when I heard the news. These four months had been so stressful. I had had to juggle family problems, my degree and talk of marriage for four months and it had completely drained me. A social worker picked up the children and we said goodbye happily.

Thoughts of my future were pushed to the forefront of my mind in February when Rayya bounded into my room excitedly.

I looked up from my textbook.

"I need to talk to you," she said with a big smile.

"Yeah?"

"We've found a guy. This *really* great guy!" she said.

I knew what she was talking about instantly. My heartbeat quickened. "What kind of guy?" I said blankly.

"What do you mean 'What kind of guy?'" she said, shaking her head. "The kind of guy who doesn't have twelve brothers and sisters. The kind of guy who has a degree from that LSE you were talking about the other day, the kind of guy who's perfect for you!"

"LSE?"

She knew she had my attention. "He's an accountant."

"An accountant?" I gulped. I would have been lucky enough if my parents had found me a guy who wasn't on the dole let alone an accountant.

"He works for some big company in Embankment. Price something..."

"What's the catch?" I asked, suspiciously.

"There is no catch. Do you want to see his photo?"

"Bet he's ugly," I said, as Rayya reached into her bag. "What!? You have it on you?" I asked incredulously. Normally, they do everything they can to prevent us from seeing a photo just in case we say no immediately. Better to get us into a position where it's difficult to say no, like after a personal meeting with him and thirty members of his immediate family.

Casually, she handed the picture to me. I reached for it tentatively.

Half of me hoped he was ugly which would make it easy to say no to and the other half hoped he was gorgeous. I was torn between Zahid and my family, between what I wanted and the prospect of losing my father's respect. I couldn't take a step away from Zahid and if this guy was horrible, it would be easy to say no. On the other hand, I was scared stiff that I would say no to a good proposal in the hopes of getting married to Zahid, which was likely to never happen. If this accountant was wonderful and brilliant then maybe I *could* build a life with him; maybe I could accept my parent's choice. I could get rid of all the uncertainty I felt when thinking about my future. I took a deep breath and looked at the picture and felt… Well, I felt nothing. He was attractive: dark hair, deep eyes, nice skin. As I looked at the picture, 'beauty is only skin deep' came to mind and I truly understood how right that was. Here was this guy - *very* good looking - but the prospect of spending the rest of my life with him, knowing nothing about him whatsoever, was scary. How could this be right?

"Well?" asked Rayya. "I think Jasmine's words were 'Delicious, can I have him for myself?'" She laughed, trying to glean my reaction.

"He's, uh, he's nice," I stammered.

"Nice? Nice! He's downright delectable! 'Nice' she says!" I couldn't complain to her. I couldn't say how I felt about this whole process because at the end of the day, she had been through it. She had said yes to a guy she saw from across a big room and had now been married to him for ten years. She was happy but we can't all be lucky, right?

"So will you meet him?" she asked.

"Uh, I'll… "

"Yes? Okay, good. We'll arrange it. Excellent!" Her eyes gleamed with excitement. I nodded dumbly and off she went, taking the photo with her.

I immediately called Zahid but his phone went straight to voice mail. I paced my room and tried to relax. *It's just a viewing. It's no big deal,* I told myself. An hour later, I called Zahid again.

"Hello?" he answered.

"Where were you?" I asked impatiently.

"When?"

"For the past hour. I tried calling you over five times."

"I was busy."

"Doing what?"

"Just chilling out with Alina."

"Why was your phone switched off?"

"It wasn't."

"Zahid, I tried calling you over five times and it kept going to voicemail so either it was switched off or you were on the phone."

"Yeah, I was on the phone."

"But you just said you were chilling out with your niece."

"I was for the past few minutes but before that I was on the phone."

"With who? Why are you acting strange?"

"I'm not acting strange. What's wrong with you?"

"Who were you on the phone with?" I repeated.

"Kieran, why are you so wound up?"

"Zahid, answer my question."

I heard him sigh resignedly. "Tasneem. We were just catching up."

Immediately, I felt the anger rise. He knew how his friendship with her made me feel. "Well you may like to know that whilst you were off *catching up* with that bitch, they've been arranging my wedding," I said.

"Kieran, firstly, calm down okay? You don't need to call her that."

"Is that all you have to say?"

"No, all I'm saying is, you don't have to take that tone with me and you don't have to go and call Tasneem a bitch. She has nothing to do with whatever's going on."

"'Whatever's going on'? Zahid, they're sorting out a guy to come and see me and it's serious!" I yelled.

"I get that but it still doesn't give you a reason to act like this," he replied.

"What's wrong with you?"

"What's wrong with *you?*" he countered.

"Fine. If it's not a big deal to you then fine. I don't know why but I thought that it may concern you." "Kieran!" I heard just as I slammed the phone down.

"Fucking prick!" I yelled. "Fucking prick!" They were right. My parents were right. I should settle down with someone who I wasn't passionate about; someone who I could build a comfortable life with; someone who wouldn't make me crazy every time he did something wrong. What the hell was wrong with him? I was fuming as I put the phone back on my desk. What a fucking prick. Here I was, telling him that they were sorting out my wedding and he was defending his goddamned *girl friend.* The bastard couldn't care less. *I'll give him something to worry about.*

The viewing was arranged for the immediate weekend. Zahid had tried to talk to me but I was still angry with his reaction at the news. I was fed up with never being able to contact him when I needed to. I couldn't help but feel like I was at the bottom of his list of priorities. We had another argument the night before the viewing, which wasn't entirely a bad thing since it took my mind off what was to happen the next day.

I woke up the next morning and felt a flurry of butterflies in my stomach. *Nothing will happen unless you want it to,* I told myself, though I wasn't entirely convinced. My family already loved this guy. He had all the makings of a perfect husband and son-in-law. If I said no to him, I knew they would all pressure me to reconsider.

As we approached ground zero, my sisters dressed me up in a simple but pretty *Shalwar Kameez* and put light make-up on my face to make my skin look naturally flawless. A few simple pieces of jewellery were also added to 'complete the look' and then I was ready. When I was told that the 'potential' had arrived, I wanted to bolt from the house or shrink up in my skin. I did not want to be here in this situation but I was going to have to swallow my nerves and just get through it.

"Don't worry, it'll only be a few minutes," said Jasmine, as we hovered outside the door.

"That's exactly what I'm worried about," I replied. How could you make a life-changing decision in only a few minutes?

"Come on," she said.

I took a deep breath and walked into the room. I felt dizzy and sick and sweaty. I visualised my shiny forehead and my shiny nose as I sat down with my eyes lowered. I fought the urge to look up at him.

"Kieran, this is Sarfraz. Sarfraz, this is Kieran," said Jasmine.

I glanced up and nodded in acknowledgement. My first impression was that he was big. Not big as in fat but big as in MAN. He looked to be about 5'10" to my 5'1". I swallowed hard. Here is this man who I'm being set up with. I'm still a girl, a little kid by comparison. How could I get married to this grown-up man and be all grown-up myself? How did I let myself get into this situation? I pushed the rising sickness back into the pit of my stomach and steeled myself for a better look. The photo had shown him to be very good-looking but people always looked different in the flesh. I glanced up again. He was tall with dark eyes and a darker complexion than mine but I never was one to care about complexion. He had thick glossy hair and the lightest hint of stubble. He *was* good-looking, a little too good-looking for my tastes, in fact. As I've said before, a woman's boyfriend/husband should never be prettier than her and this guy was definitely better-looking than me. My parents had chosen well.

"So I hear you study at Queen Mary," he said in a warm, deep voice.

I nodded but then looked up and said, "Yes." This was no time to be a shrinking violet. Obviously, you were supposed to be coy and shy but this is my *life* we're talking about here and I'm not about to let someone else do all the talking. "I hear you work in Embankment," I said.

He smiled slightly and said, "Yes."

Jasmine acted like her hem was the most interesting thing in the world.

"So do you enjoy your study?" he asked.

"Yes. And you? Do you enjoy your work?"

"Well, as much as one can enjoy accounting," he said with an easy laugh.

I smiled in return and tried to relax a bit. *Shit shit shit shit shit shit shit*... that's what was going through my mind. *What am I doing? What do I do?*

"So, Sarfraz," said Jasmine, breaking the awkward silence. "What are your life plans? What do you intend to do after marriage?"

"Well, once we're married," he said, glancing at me, "I wouldn't mind if my wife wanted to work. We would obviously have to stay at my family home for a while, make sure that my younger brother can look after my mother. Then I would like to get a mortgage, buy a house of my own, the usual things." He referred to his mother rather than his parents because his father had passed away when he was fifteen.

"And how many children would you like?" asked Jasmine. I gulped hard at Jasmine's boldness but he wasn't fazed.

"Well, that is up to Allah," he said, smiling winningly. He turned his attention back to me. "What about you Kieran? What are your life plans?" he asked.

"Similar to yours," I said. "Marriage, house, children." I looked down. What should I do? Do I sell myself to him? Do I make myself out to be an unmarriageable monster? What if Zahid and I just never work out? We have so many arguments and deep down I knew that I could never face my father over Zahid.

"And what about ambitions for yourself rather than for your family?" he asked with a challenging stare.

I didn't like the way he was looking at me, like I was some docile female who possessed none of her own thoughts. I met his glare.

"What I want," I said, "is to admit my mistake in studying Computer Science instead of law at university, to study for my CPE and LPC at BPP London, complete my training contract and make partner at Freshfields Bruckhaus Deringer by the time I'm thirty," I finished angrily. "But of course, if my *husband* wants me to stay at home and look after the kids, that would be fine also."

Jasmine balled her hands into small fists and I could feel her squirm beside me. I continued to glare at Sarfraz but instead of bewilderment or disparagement, there was a look of approval on his face.

He broke out in a big smile and said, "Good. I'm going to say yes. I hope you do too."

At that, almost as if it was scripted, his uncle came in to break up the meeting. After a few minutes exchanging pleasantries with his family, Jasmine and I got up and left. My heart was pounding. What the hell was that?

Jasmine squealed as quietly as possible. "Oh my God, I *love* him!" she exclaimed. I didn't know what to think. Truthfully, I was impressed. And relieved. And scared. I knew that I would not get another proposal like this one but at the same time, how could I possibly say yes when I hadn't even spent five minutes in his presence?

"Well? What do you think?" asked Jasmine, turning to me excitedly.

"Erm, I… "

"You liked him right? 'I'm going to say yes, I hope you do too.' Now that's a man!"

It *was* nice how he had just admitted straight up what he was thinking.

"Well?" she prompted.

"Yeah, he's nice," I replied.

"'Yeah, he's nice but no' or 'yeah, he's nice and yes?'"

"I don't know, I need time to think."

"Come on, Kieran, first instinct. Yes or no? Yes or no?"

I shrugged. "Well, first instinct is yes but - "

"Yes!" she yelled. "You don't know how lucky you are."

I nodded and held back tears.

Count yourself lucky, I told myself countless times after that day but security and comfort cannot replace love. I had to give up on Zahid. As dark a thought that it was, the only way I could marry Zahid was if my father passed away. Only then, would I have the courage to face my family over it. There was no way I could lose my father's respect, not over Zahid. I couldn't. And that was it. My choice but not my choice: arranged, not forced. A decision based on the fear of not being able to get what I really wanted. Official confirmations were exchanged, the date was set for June and preparations began immediately.

I floated like a ghost through the first week after saying yes. I had called Zahid immediately after the meeting. How do you tell someone something like that?

I simply said, "I said yes," which was met with a full minute's silence.

"Zahid?" I asked tentatively.

"Why so soon?" he asked. "Kieran, we're in our final year at university. Why are they arranging it now? Why so soon? Why did you say yes? Kieran, why didn't you say no?" he asked.

I didn't know what to say.

"Why?" he asked quietly.

"Because everyone liked him."

"And you?"

"I… I didn't know what to do."

"You didn't know what to do!? Say no? You couldn't say no?"

"I… they all liked him, Zahid," I repeated.

"Fuck them!" he screamed. "Fuck them! Kieran, what the hell have you done? Kieran, *I* was going to look after you. You haven't given me a chance. We can sort it out. Kieran, you gotta tell them no. We can sort it out."

"And say what Zahid? That I'm holding out for a five percent chance that I may be able to marry you? That I'm holding out for something better? What happens next year when your parents say no? You think a guy like this comes along every day for people like me?"

"What's so fucking special about him? Huh? Kieran? Answer me!"

"I don't know. I… "

"Give me some time, Kieran. That's all I'm asking for. We will finish our degrees, get past all this. We'll be together. You don't get it Kieran. Everything, it doesn't matter. I don't care, you're the one Kieran. You are. What the hell am I supposed to do without you? I can't let you be someone else's wife." His voice started to quiver and I bit back my own tears.

"Zahid, I'm too scared," I said.

"Don't be, Kieran. We're gonna get through this. Just say no and we'll sort it out."

"I can't Zahid. It's all going ahead."

"How could you say yes? You didn't even talk to me about it. Do you realise that we're going to see each other every day for the next four months? What were you thinking?"

"I don't know… it just happened. I, I can't live on 'maybe'."

"I'll give you 'definitely'," he cried. "Kieran, I'll give you 'definitely'. I'm not kidding. Please, please, you don't understand."

"I can't, I can't," I said with tears streaming down my face. "I have to go."

"Kieran, no," he said but I hung up. I placed the phone on my desk, walked over to my door and calmly locked it. I then slid down the wall to the floor and wept.

The final four months of my university education went faster than I had expected. I struggled through the completion of countless pieces of coursework and my final-year project whilst trying my best to avoid Zahid. My revision was worse than for any set of exams I had sat in the past. One day, when trying to revise for one of my exams, I walked over to Ashley who was on one of the PCs in the ITL.

"GlaxoSmithKline," I read over her shoulder. "What are you up to?"

"Oh, just applying to their bloody graduate training scheme," she replied.

"Oh, right. Shouldn't you be concentrating on the exams? If you don't get decent grades, you're not gonna get on any scheme."

"Hmm… I know. I've been trying to but I just can't be arsed. I've had enough of the whole thing," she said.

"Well, there's not long to go now," I said.

"I know, you're right and applying to these bloody training schemes is probably pointless. They make you go to those bloody assessment centres where they make you do everything but sing and dance."

"I know exactly what you mean."

"You're lucky you don't have to go through it anymore," she said.

"I suppose so."

"You don't sound convinced."

"No, I am. It's just that I can't help but feel that doing this whole degree was a bit pointless if I'm not going to get a job at the end of it. I am glad I did because I've always wanted to go to university and get a degree but now I'm pretty sure I'm gonna feel useless after we graduate."

"Hey, if I had a husband who could afford to take care of me, I would not be complaining about it. I reckon I could get used to being a lady of leisure!" she said.

I sighed in response.

"Kieran, if you're not convinced, you can always get a job later on. You said yourself that he liked the fact that you have ambition. It's just that you can't have a job straight after, isn't it?"

"Yeah, I know. It's just that I feel like I've lost all my drive now. Like 'What's the point?' but you're right, I'm not going to complain about it."

"Ok, good. Now get your butt back to revision." I smiled wryly and walked away.

The exams came and went in a blur and before I knew it, it was all over. On the day that the results were due, I received an e-mail from Alinoor. He was the brainiest guy in our year and also part of my inner circle of friends at university. The e-mail briefly stated that he had hacked into the Examination Officer's web space and had obtained a copy of the results before they were actually posted. *Please be aware that though unlikely, results MAY have changed from this,* he wrote, covering his ass I assumed.

Shit! I thought as I double-clicked on the attached HTML file. I dug out my student number and followed the list down to 002377311. I held my breath. Next to it in tiny font there was a '1'. I swallowed hard and tried to contain the rush of relief. *They may change,* I chanted in my head. That afternoon, the real file confirmed the '1'. I had achieved a First. A First Class degree from the University of London. I did not know of one other Bengali girl from Tower Hamlets who had done that. I whooped with joy and let all my sisters know.

I did not make a point of telling my parents. Firstly, because they would not really know or appreciate the difference between a First Class and anything else and secondly, because my mother probably would not believe me. I remember getting my GCSE grades and when I told everyone that I had obtained seven As out of eleven subjects, they were all happy but my mother did not say anything. A week later, Javed had paid us one of his rare visits. She heard Javed say "Seven As!" disbelievingly and immediately took on a look of triumph.

"She was lying?" said my mother. "I knew she was lying."

"No," said Javed. "That's really good. I just couldn't believe it, that's all." My mother made a defiant grunt and went on about her work. I really did not understand what was going through her head but that really got to me. *Five years of studying versus one word,* I thought. One word from her son could discredit all that I had worked for. Once again, it pushed my mother's favouritism to the forefront of my life.

My brothers never did anything the hard way. On that same visit, whilst my mother fussed around Javed, he mentioned that he was going to get a degree.

"Seriously? You're gonna go back to uni?" I asked.

"No, I'm changing my name."

"You what?" I said, confused.

"My mate still does security at the College of Law. He can access the database with the list of students who have a degree from there. He's gonna pick out a name for me and I'm going to change my name," he said.

"You can't do that."

"Why not?"

"Coz it's not that simple."

"What's not simple about it?"

"I don't know. But if it was that simple, everyone would do it."

"Not everyone has access to their database," he said proudly.

"You never want to do anything the hard way, do you?" I said, dismissing his crazy idea.

"No, I'm being serious. My mate gets a name from the database. I change my name with deed poll and when I apply for jobs, if they go back and check, I'll be there."

"That's silly. If you want a degree so much, you should just go and do it."

"It's not just that. It wipes my record clean. No criminal record under the new name. No bad credit report, no debt, just a clean slate."

"But it's not as easy as that. Don't you think that when they do a search on you, your original name comes up? Otherwise, every criminal in the world would be doing it."

"No, it's worth doing, trust me."

"But surely, when the debt people look for a Javed Ali, it will point them towards your new name. It's just your name that changes. You're still who you are."

"No, I'm gonna create everything under my new name; passport, bank account, ID, everything and then when I'm ready, Javed Ali will just disappear and I'm gonna become the new name."

"You're crazy," I said before turning back to my cereal.

These are the actions of the man my mother would sooner trust than believe that I could do well in life. So instead of telling her I got a First and expecting words of congratulations, I did not bother telling her at all.

After my initial celebration, I began to wonder what Zahid had achieved.

I had done my best to avoid him these past four months but inevitably our paths had crossed and each time, it broke another piece of my heart and weakened my resolve to ignore him. One such occasion had arisen the day before my last exam. Zahid found me on the top floor of the deserted ITL late one evening. "Kieran," he pleaded. "What's going on? You don't answer my calls. You avoid me like the plague. Why?"

"Why do you think, Zahid?" I replied. "Don't you get it? I care about you. When I see you, all I want is to be with you. I want things to go back to the way they were more than anything but this isn't a fairy tale. Things happen. Things change. And being around you is dangerous."

He took a step closer. "Why?" he asked tenderly.

"Zahid, I have to go," I said, turning away but he blocked my exit.

"Why?" He searched my eyes.

I caught my breath. I had spent so much time avoiding his eyes that I had forgotten their depth and power. He was so beautiful. And he wanted me so desperately. I loved him so much. I couldn't imagine being without him. I leaned into him and he caught me and wrapped me in his arms. He held me so tight as I pushed myself deep into him. He was so warm and so safe, it made me want to cry.

"Kieran, you have to be mine," he said softly.

I shook my head and pulled away from him. "No," I said with tears in my eyes. I packed up my stuff and fled down the stairs. That was the last time I had spoken to him.

I avoided him throughout graduation and despite it being a fantastic day, one of the best and proudest of my life, I felt a tinge of sadness every time I looked at him. If I was going marry Sarfraz, I wanted to do things right with a clean slate. Now I looked forward. I had a First Class degree and Sarfraz seemed like someone who would encourage ambition; indeed, that was the reason he had said yes to marrying me. I had been in contact with him a few times but because we were not officially engaged, any contact at all was frowned upon. The few times I had spoken to him, he seemed easy-going and sweet. I asked myself if he was someone I could have fallen in love with if I had not met Zahid first. The answer was, "Maybe."

Chapter 7. Preparation

"Mm, tastes good," said Shelly.

"Are you just saying that?" I frowned.

"No really, it's good." She chewed on a piece of chicken. I had been learning to cook for the past month and my latest dish, chicken curry, was being taste-tested by Shelly and Neha.

"No, it's not bad," said Neha. "It's a bit salty but other than that, it's okay."

I picked at my curry-stained nails and drooped. "It's disgusting, isn't it?" I asked.

"No!" they both cried in unison.

I shook my head and threw my hands in the air.

"You'll get better, trust me," said Shelly. "Practice makes perfect."

"Oh, I'll have plenty of time to practise when living with the in-laws! You guys are lucky you don't have to deal with all of that," I said.

"Oh, come on!" said Shelly. "Your husband-to-be is this gorgeous, educated accountant who is RICH and you're complaining!" She poked me with her finger.

"No, I know but… "

"But what?" said Neha, coming towards me with a wooden spoon.

"Yeah what?" asked Shelly, picking up a metal spoon. They both advanced towards me with mock menace.

"Nooo!" I yelled and ran out of the kitchen. They chased after me into the living room and pretended to beat me with the spoons as I lay on the sofa. "I can't help it if I have the best husband!" I yelled.

They both laughed and collapsed onto the sofa on top of me.

"Oh, you have the best husband do you? Do you?" yelled Shelly swinging the spoon above me.

"Hey, I'm just agreeing with you guys!" I yelled. The door bell rang and we quickly stood up and straightened our shalwar kameezes. I rushed to the door and opened it to a neighbour. "Asalam Alaikum," I said, as the woman walked in. I called my mother and left the woman to her own devices.

I cleaned up the kitchen whilst humming to myself quietly. I smiled as I thought of Sarfraz. I was going to give it my best shot. He seemed like a really decent guy and who knows? Maybe my parents had done something right by me for a change. My dad seemed really happy and I suppose that made it all worth it. I didn't taste the chicken curry as I placed it on the table. Maybe it wouldn't *all* be a picture of domestic bliss but I was going to do this wholeheartedly.

The next two weeks were spent preparing for the wedding. The invitations, wedding gold, outfits, venue and catering were sorted out one-by-one and the date began to creep closer until June 8th was only a few days away. I felt slightly sick when I thought about it but it was not as bad as I had predicted. I was calm and collected. I spent my days in a whirlwind of preparation and my nights pushing thoughts of Zahid away. Part of me regretted not having had sex with him. We were so close that it would have been as painless as possible. I couldn't imagine getting close to Sarfraz let alone having sex with him! He was a good-looking guy and there was an attraction there but it was nothing compared to what I felt for Zahid. Zahid was laughter and craziness and passion. I convinced myself that passion was over-rated and that it was much better settling for a guy who could look after me. I was determined not to let my feelings for Zahid get in the way of my marriage to Sarfraz.

Saturday 7th June 2003

I woke up and felt light and airy, which was weird since I had gone to sleep the night before expecting to wake up with a heavy heart. This was it. This was the single most important thing that was ever going to happen to me. I suddenly wished that I had taken more advantage of the four month gap between meeting Sarfraz and our wedding day by getting to know him better. I had been so busy getting my final project and revision done that my impending marriage had sort of been pushed to the side. Now that it was crunch time, I just couldn't get my head round it.

My sisters awoke at 7.30 a.m. "What have you done?" was the first thing Sania asked.

"What do you mean?"

"I told you yesterday that you had to get your sleep. You didn't get your eight hours like I said, did you?"

"Why do you say that?" I asked.

"The monstrous bags under your eyes!"

"Oh my God!" I gasped in mock horror. "I can't do this, let's call off the wedding! I have *bags* under my eyes!"

Sania laughed.

"I'm sure this is highly amusing to you all," I said and indeed it was. I hardly wore any make-up and wasn't one to dress up and wear jewellery. In fact, before this wedding, I hadn't even possessed one piece of jewellery. All through my teens, my sisters had joked that they would have a nightmare dressing me up on my wedding day since I'd insist that I was wearing too much makeup/jewellery/bright colours, etc.

I managed to get through the plucking and prodding without any tears, though the mascara stick poking my eyeball because I couldn't keep my eyes open almost bought tears. "Don't let them fall! They'll smudge your eyes!" cried my sisters. I blinked the tears back until the state of my mascara was officially declared safe. I couldn't believe it was happening. Today was my Mehndi, which translates as 'Henna', the thick dark mixture used as a cosmetic dye, a little like a temporary tattoo. Henna tattoos had been made popular by Madonna but had been used for years at Asian weddings. The Mehndi was usually on a Saturday before the wedding which was usually on a Sunday.

My Mehndi was being staged at a local youth club, hardly the classiest of locations but my sisters had decorated it in a way that made it look really nice. I felt a little nervous as they wrapped the gleaming pink sari around my body. Usually the colour theme of a Mehndi is green to coincide with the green colour of the wet Henna and so the bride-to-be is dressed in green. My sisters, however, had insisted that I would look 'beautiful and stunning' in this pink creation. Finally, they bought a mirror so I could look at myself. They all stood beaming as I stepped in front of it.

Mascara and kohl were my sworn enemies. Throughout my teens, I had refused to pick up a stick of eyeliner but now as I stared at myself, I could understand why my girlfriends used them religiously.

"Jeez, you guys really have the ugly-ducking-turned-swan thing down to a T," I remarked.

"Kieran! Is that all you can say?" said Sania.

I turned to look at my smiling sisters and blinked back tears. "Thank you, guys. It's perfect," I said with shaking hands and a quivering voice.

"Okay!" exclaimed Jasmine. "No time to get emotional, we have a schedule to keep to. We have to be at the hall by three."

I nodded by moving my head as little as possible. The face and jewellery was all so perfect, I didn't want to mess them up by jostling something out of place.

"You guys have to watch me. You know what I'm like. I'll reach up to rub my eye without thinking and - "

"Don't you dare!" said Shelly. "I'll be watching you like a hawk!"

"Come on beautiful, let's get going," said Jasmine to Sania. She was the youngest but probably the vainest and had spent more time looking in the mirror today than the rest of us put together. She also had a huge complex about the colour of her skin. She was slightly darker than the rest of my sisters. In Bengali culture, the beauty of a woman is often judged by how fair she is. My mother was extremely fair for an Asian woman and had passed this trait onto most of us. An elder auntie had once commented to Sania, "The rest of your sisters are so fair, what happened to you?" and ever since then, she had been paranoid about it. She tucked a stray hair behind her ear and ignored Jasmine's command.

Shelly squeezed my arms and said, "It'll be a good day."

I nodded in response.

"Okay, the camera is ready," said Jasmine "Let's show them some magic!" She grabbed Sania and put her by my side. As the only unmarried sister, Sania was responsible for staying by my side whilst the camera was running.

I took a deep breath. I wanted to shrivel up or run away but I had made this decision and I had to see it through. But this wasn't the kind of thing you 'see through'. It wasn't just an obstacle in life; it wasn't a temporary state which you had to survive; it was walking into marriage - something that is meant to last a lifetime. My heart quickened as I stepped out the door. I lowered my eyes as Sania held my arm and lead me towards the stairs. The cameras were already rolling. I felt hot and sweaty under the glare and already wished that the day was over. We descended the stairs slowly and walked out to the car. All my neighbours were outside milling around and stared at me as I got into the car as gracefully as I could.

Once inside, I breathed a little. "Shouldn't all of these people already be at the hall?" I asked my sisters.

"Don't worry about them," said Jasmine.

The ride to the hall was bumpy and I held my hair in place. It was done-up in an intricate do which wouldn't be seen, however, because the sari was covering my hair. I felt sick. I hadn't been able to eat and now my stomach felt unsettled. I tried to calm myself and wondered, if this was how nervous I was today, how would I feel tomorrow? I pushed the thoughts from my mind and concentrated on small things like not smudging my make-up and keeping my sari as crease-free as possible.

When we got to the hall, there were what seemed like hundreds of people milling around. As soon as the news got out that I had arrived, more and more people began to come out. I groaned inwardly. I hated crowds but mostly I hated being in the spotlight. I hated people staring at me and judging me.

We exited the car and entered the hall. The clamour died down for a second. I felt like Cinderella but then remembered that Cinderella *does* end up with her Prince Charming and I definitely wasn't going to. I took my place upon the stage and squirmed under the glare of my female relatives. I spotted three of my best friends among the crowd and almost stood up and waved. I smiled to them and beckoned subtly for them to come over.

"Kieran!" started Rabika. "Oh, my God. You look stunning."

I shook my head modestly.

"God, you look beautiful," said Rita, staring at me. "Who did the makeup? It's flawless!"

"A beautician. She's one of Shelly's friends so she gave us a freebie," I replied.

"Oh, my God, you have to keep in touch with her. She has to do my wedding," said Rashanara.

I nodded.

"How are you feeling?" asked Rabika.

"It's all kind of surreal," I replied. We turned our attention to the cameramen who were setting up their equipment in front of me. My friends took a step back. "Stay close today, okay?" I told them and they all nodded as they went back to their places.

And so it began. First, the guests were fed rice, meat, samosas, salad and then cake. I watched them eat and talk and laugh. The majority of the women in the room had been through what I was going through so I wasn't going to feel sorry for myself. Then, one by one, my friends and family came and fed me either a small piece of fruit or a spoonful of cake, all on camera. I took tiny bites of the food and tried not to look straight at the camera. The heat and glare of the light had given me a headache. I had skin that became greasy very quickly so I silently prayed that I still looked fresh.

"You look beautiful," said one of my cousins as she squeezed my arm.

"Thank you," I replied, taking a bite out of the cake she was feeding me. She kissed me on the cheek and off she went. It was finally time for the Mehndi to be put on my hands. Neha sat down next to me and smiled. Another running joke between my sisters was the fact that I hated Mehndi. I never wore it for Eid or weddings and so this was all a bit of a nightmare for me. Neha and one of my friends did a hand each. They drew tiny intricate patters - flowers and spirals and all things pretty. I sat as still as possible.

Half way through their work, I joked, "I have a wedgie." They shook their heads and laughed.

"Only you would make such a joke at a time like this," commented Neha and went back to her work. The camera zoomed in on my hands after they had finished. People ooh-ed and ahh-ed at how lovely I looked and how beautiful the Mehndi had turned out to be. I smiled and acted the perfect coy woman but silently wished that the day would go faster.

At 6 p.m., guests slowly began to leave. When it was finally time to leave, I heaved a sigh of relief. I was tired, sleepy and sweaty. All I wanted to do was go home, take off all the wedding regalia, have a cold shower and go to sleep in my comfy PJs. My shoulders ached, my head thumped and my stomach churned.

As soon as we were home and away from the guests, I switched back into 'Kieran Mode'.

"AMA!" I yelled down the stairs to my mother. "Is there enough hot water for a shower?"

"Yes!" she called back.

"Cool," I said as I unwrapped the pink sari from my body. I stretched luxuriously, something I hadn't been able to do all day. I wrapped a towel around myself like a shawl over my blouse and petticoat and ran to the bathroom.

I let the cool water calm my churning mind and tried to relax. I flexed my shoulders and yawned. I couldn't wait to hit the bed. I dried off, dressed and popped into the living room. "I'm going to sleep," I declared to my sisters who were strewn about on the sofas.

"You can't do that!" exclaimed Sania. "Your hair will be a jungle tomorrow if you sleep on it while it's wet!"

"What are your straighteners for?" I asked nonchalantly and walked off.

My stomach was still doing flip-flops when I climbed into bed. As I reached for my phone to set the alarm for tomorrow, I noticed that I had a missed call. My stomach leapt as Zahid's name flashed up on the screen. I felt sick. He knew I was getting married tomorrow and I had told him to leave me alone, to let me go, hundreds of times. What the hell was he doing calling me the night before my wedding? I silenced the phone then got out of bed and placed the phone on my desk on the opposite side of the room. Tomorrow was going to be hard enough without thoughts of Zahid thrown into the mix. As I lay down, I thought it would take me ages to get to sleep but instead, I drifted off to a dreamless sleep within minutes.

The next day, I woke before the alarm went off. I got up and looked in the mirror. Just as Sania had predicted, my hair was a tangled mess. I groaned at the sight of the dark circles around my eyes. Almost immediately, my stomach started to do those familiar flip-flops - a mixture of adrenaline and nerves like the feeling you get just before a drop on a rollercoaster. I had been so caught up in the wedding preparations that week that I didn't really know what I felt about it all. I sat on my bed for a moment of reflection. *Check me out on my Buddha trip,* I thought as I breathed in and out to calm myself. *Am I okay about this?* I was scared, no, *terrified* of it all. I was scared about my future. I was scared of Sarfraz's family and I was scared of him. I felt like I was losing control over my life. Like I was just handing it over to someone and saying, "Do what you will." *Okay, I'm rambling. Breathe. Breathe. Breathe.*

My mind wandered to Zahid. Marrying him would have been so perfect. I used to envisage us moving into a new home and fighting over who should do the painting and him playfully scolding me for using our hose pipe during the water ban and teasing me about my bad cooking. Now, all these hopes had turned to dust. I was marrying a complete stranger. I consoled myself by thinking about Sarfraz's good points. He too was good-looking and smart. Whether or not he was sweet or funny like Zahid remained to be seen and of course, I had plenty of time to find out after today. *I'm okay,* I told myself. Girls went through this all the time. It was just my time. And I was okay.

I was practising my china doll look in front of the mirror (just the right mixture of sweet and sorrow) when I heard a knock at my door. I opened it and was faced with a huge bunch of flowers.

"What?" I started as Sania's head poked out from behind the huge bouquet of white roses. "What is this?" I asked with a bemused smile. I had only ever received flowers once before in my life (from a friend on my birthday) and I was thrilled as I took them from her.

"Read the card," she said.

Kieran, don't worry. I'm nervous too. We'll laugh at this day for years to come. I promise.

My heart did a somersault as I read the signature on the card: *Sarfraz.*

"Isn't he amazing!?" squealed Sania. "My God, I love him," she said, charging into my room. "These flowers are gorgeous and what he wrote… so sweet!"

I was rather taken aback by his gesture. I was flattered and felt an instant bond with him. I felt slightly relieved and was glad to know he was feeling the way I was.

"I'll get a vase and ooh, I gotta tell the rest!" said Sania and ran out in a whirlwind. It wasn't long before the rest of my sisters filed into my room. They all gasped at the flowers and smiled at the message.

"Jeez, you guys, you're all more in love with him than I am!" I said.

"Of course," declared Jasmine. "He's lovely. If only my husband was more like that!"

"The most romantic thing mine ever did was get me a portion of chips in Bangladesh!" said Shelly as she breathed in the scent of the roses.

"They are pretty," I commented.

"Oh! He got to *her* too. Don't try to hide it, Kieran. He got you!" said Shelly.

A smile began to creep into the corner of my mouth and then spread into laughter. My sisters all laughed with me.

"He seems like a good guy," I said and they all nodded in agreement.

Before long, the house was alive with guests, relatives and children buzzing around. Shelly's friend, the beautician, had thankfully been on time and had set to work on me at 12 p.m. I wasn't due at the hall until 1.30 p.m. so there was plenty of time. Just as the finishing touches were being put to my face, I heard a commotion downstairs. Sania ran into the room.

"What's going on?" I asked, alarmed.

"Kamal, that bastard, is shouting," said Sania.

"Why?"

"He asked Dad for twenty quid but Dad said no and he started to yell."

"What about all the people there?" I asked.

"He doesn't care!"

"What's he saying?"

"All sorts of crap. That Dad's spending thousands on your wedding but can't give him twenty quid and -"

"What?" I interrupted, furious at what she told me. "How dare he? Dad gives him twenty quid practically every day. He's probably stolen twice as much from Dad than what's being spent on this wedding."

"Calm down, Kieran," said Shelly who was sitting placidly on the bed. "You're going to ruin your make-up."

I shook my head angrily. "I mean for one day! He can't just shut up for one bloody day!" I tried to calm myself. I don't know why I got so angry; it was always the same routine and this was nothing new. I just thought that the day should be as drama-free as possible since it was the biggest day of my so-called life!

I paced the room angrily and my sisters did their best to calm me. Shelly's friend quickly touched up my make-up and then dressed me in the glittering red sari. By the time she was finished, I looked the perfect bride. I was still angry at what was happening downstairs but reminded myself that it was the last day I would have to spend here in the family house. It couldn't get much worse than here. I touched wood as the thought passed through my mind. I looked at myself in the mirror approvingly: long long lashes, fair fair skin and deep dark eyes. I hoped Sarfraz would appreciate all this.

The ride to the hall was bumpier and more nerve-wracking than yesterday's. I tried to relax as my sisters chattered happily in the back of the lush limousine. As we parked up outside York Hall, I felt sick. This was it. No turning back now. I got out of the car slowly and felt a headache form as the camera started rolling. We inched our way into the hall and I was seated in the women's section of the hall.

Let the games begin, I thought. As soon I sat down, a group of men descended into the area around me. It was time for my *Nikah* - the official act of unifying a man and woman in an Islamic marriage. Usually it was done before the wedding day but on this occasion, it had been left for the big day.

The *Mehsab* read out the Islamic verse *(Sura)* which solemnised my marriage to Sarfraz. I was meant to reply *Khabul* which means 'I accept'. But I was told by Rayya not to accept straight after the reading of the Sura, as doing so would be deemed as "giving yourself away too easily." An auntie sitting next to me pinched me gently after an appropriate length of time had passed. I took a deep breath and, almost inaudibly, said, "Khabul."

Immediately, the crowd disbanded. My heart slammed in my chest. That was it. I was officially married. I breathed deeply to calm myself and to relieve the tension that was growing between my shoulder blades.

After the Nikah, the food was served. I watched as the caterers rushed around placing huge dishes of tandoori chicken on the tables. I watched people eat voraciously. I was told to eat but I really wasn't hungry. I picked at the rice that was placed in front of me. After the meal, the caterers tidied up around the guests. An air of excitement grew on my side of the hall as it was time to bring Sarfraz round to my side of the hall and seat him next to me. I felt the knot in my stomach tighten as I watched the procession approach.

The theme music to 'The Godfather' rang in my ears and I tried to hear through it. I watched as they came closer and sat still as Sarfraz was seated next to me. We exchanged golden decorated necklaces. A bride is meant to keep her gaze lowered as a sign of modesty and respect but I couldn't help but let my eyes flicker up to meet his. I immediately looked down again but not before catching the hint of a smile in his eyes. My head was buzzing and it seemed like there were thousands, not hundreds, of people in the building. Relatives deposited gifts, namely gold jewellery and money onto the table in front of us.

Then it was time to pay respects to the elders of our respective families. This involved reaching down and touching the feet of the elder and then touching one's chest in quick succession three times. It was called giving them your *Salaam.* It was a Bengali tradition that had been adopted from our Indian counterparts. Through reading, I had discovered that this was an un-Islamic practice. The only person/entity we were meant to worship was Allah and kneeling down to touch the feet of a human was a form of human worship. I had bought this to the attention of my parents before the wedding but they had said it was a cultural tradition that had to be obeyed and so it was.

After all the exchanges, it was time for the *Bidai*: The Goodbye. It was the part I had been dreading. The Goodbye was meant to be a big emotional scene where the bride clings to her mother and cries her eyes out because she does not want to leave her family. But I never cried in public and of course, I felt nothing for my mother, so any act of love towards her would be forced and awkward. I was sad but a part of me was glad to be finally leaving the family. I had been through so much pain at that house and to be finally able to say goodbye to it was liberating. For all I knew, I could have been walking from one nightmare into another but Sarfraz seemed like a good man and I knew that things had to get better.

We walked out of the hall slowly. Sarfraz entered the car first. My sisters started to cry which was good because it started me off too. It wasn't the done thing for a bride to skip out happily, wave to her family and jump into the car, so when I felt the emotion well up inside, I was relieved. I got the hug with my mother over and done with and then spent a while saying goodbye to my sisters. I didn't wail and scream like many a bride I had seen in the past. I simply let the tears stream down my face. This was the beginning of a new chapter of my life. I was saying goodbye to all the pain I had experienced living with my parents. I was finally free of them. I cried bittersweet tears and was helped into the car by Sania who was coming with me to Sarfraz's family home. I sat in the car and let the tears roll down.

The door opened then closed quietly. I lay still in the bed. I didn't know what to do. I wanted to face him and talk to him but I was scared stiff. Sleeping next to Zahid had been such a pleasure. Wrapping myself up in his arms had been the most natural thing in the world. Lying in this cold bed waiting for Sarfraz to enter it just left me feeling empty. I froze as I heard him walk over to my side of the bed and sit on the edge of it.

"Kieran?" he said softly. *Jesus, what am I supposed to do?* "Kieran?" he asked again. I pretended to stir and fluttered my eyes but then went back to 'sleep'. He reached out and touched my hair. "You're my wife now," he said. "You're my wife," he said again, this time as if trying out the sound of the words in his mouth. "You're beautiful, Kieran. You really are." He caressed my cheek.

What's going on? I thought to myself. *He's not trying to wake me up is he? He's not planning to have sex is he? Not on the first night!*

His voice interrupted my thoughts. "And I just want to say sorry. I'm sorry for all the things that I will do wrong. I'm sorry for not treating you the way you deserve but I will say this: I will always take care of you. I promise that I will always make sure you have the things you need." With that, he kissed my cheek and stood up. I felt him get into the bed next to me and I exhaled softly. I didn't know what to make of it but his promises had soothed me and my fears subsided. I listened to the sounds of his breathing and they lulled me into a deep sleep.

Chapter 8. Growing and Shrinking

I woke up on the morning after my wedding and my first thought was that I needed a shower. I jumped out of bed and then it hit me. I wasn't in my bed or in my house. I'd been sleeping next to a complete stranger in a strange house full of strange people. I felt sick to my stomach. I knew that Sania was here as well but I felt alone. I stood in my nightgown and just froze. I felt so out of place; almost other-worldly. What was I doing here with this strange man? Where was Zahid who made me feel so safe? I felt like the ground had been pulled from under my feet. I tried to calm myself and took a few deep breaths.

"Are you okay?" His voice startled me and I spun around. Sarfraz sat up in bed rubbing his eyes like a little boy.

I shook thoughts of Zahid away and faced Sarfraz properly. "Yes, I'm okay."

"What's the matter?" he asked gently. "You look lost." His awareness startled me a little.

"I am a little lost," I admitted.

"The bathroom is the second right," he replied.

I said nothing.

He waited a moment and then broke into a smile. "I'm kidding, I know you don't mean physically lost."

I smiled in response and felt a little warmth toward him.

"Come and sit next to me," he said.

I hesitated for a moment but then walked over and sat down. This 'Do what your husband says' thing was going to take time.

"Kieran, I can't imagine how tough this is for you; to be uprooted from your family and thrown into a place where you feel lost. It would be unnerving to even the strongest of people. It's okay to feel a little unsettled."

I felt genuinely relieved at his words. I felt relieved that I had said yes to him. And I felt a glimmer of hope that maybe one day I could grow to love him. I smiled warmly. "Thank you. That really means a lot to me."

"Okay, enough of the soppiness now go get me breakfast," he said. I looked at him sharply but caught the trace of a smile. He broke out in laughter.

"You're so evil!" I said but he just continued to laugh like a child. I shook my head at him and began to get up. He caught my arm quickly and I missed a beat. It was the first time a man had touched me since Zahid and I had broken up four months ago. I turned toward him.

"What would you like for breakfast?" he asked.

"Nothing, I'm not really hungry. I would like a shower though," I said. He pointed me in the right direction and I hurriedly had my shower before the rest of the family woke up.

Sarfraz, his younger sister Amina, Sania and I had breakfast together that morning. There were surprisingly few people around which was a good thing. Usually, neighbours crowd the house after a wedding to catch a glimpse of the bride without her public face on. Sarfraz teased Sania about her dyed jet black hair and I talked to his sister about which A-Levels she was planning to study. All in all, it wasn't a bad experience. I felt hope for the future. Things were getting better.

You hear all these horror stories about how husbands are sweet, gentle and polite at first but then turn into complete dogs after a while. Sarfraz was so sweet that I couldn't help but think he was hiding his true self; there had to be a mean streak in him somewhere. Plus all sweet all the time isn't all good, right?

The first time I saw something other than sweet was on our fifth night together. Up until then, we had cuddled a little and kissed a few times. On the fifth night however, it was obvious he wanted more. It was 11 p.m. at night and I was yawning in bed. He sat next to me and touched my arm gently. I turned to him and smiled tentatively. I knew that we had to consummate the marriage sooner or later.

Slowly he pulled me towards him. He looked at me with deep questioning eyes. I felt my heart quicken and knew that it was time. I breathed deeply and nodded almost imperceptibly. He scooped me into his arms. Inside, I was all knotted up. I couldn't believe it was about to happen. Doubt plagued my mind. Any time I had thought about this moment in the past few years, I had imagined sharing it with Zahid. I was nervous about Sarfraz not being able to enter me. I didn't even know if he was a virgin himself. The fact that he was Muslim should have been confirmation enough but you never knew these days.

I could feel how hard he was as he lay on top of me. He began to kiss me harder than he had before and I could feel the lust radiate from him. He gripped my shoulders and pulled me into him. It was strange having him touch me but in a pleasurable way. His strange, manly hands began to touch me in places they hadn't before. He lifted my nightie over my shoulders revealing the simple cotton underwear I had on. I was so nervous, I felt like I was going to faint. He leaned down and kissed my stomach, a slow lingering kiss. He moved down a little and I gasped both in anticipation and shock. *He isn't going there, is he? No way on earth!* For a moment I thought I was wrong as he went a little further but then he moved up and kissed me on the lips.

"You're so beautiful," he mumbled with dark lust-filled eyes. He kissed my neck as his hands roamed my body. "So goddamned beautiful." He slid his hands between my legs. "Do you know how much I want you? I can't believe how much I want you. I can't help myself." He grabbed me hard and began to rub himself against me. My body responded to his touch and to his words. He took off my bra and touched my breasts. He undressed quickly then pulled off my pants. He slid a finger between my legs then trailed it up my stomach. It left a small wet trail. I couldn't believe how good he was making me feel. He breathed warmly between my legs and then looked up at me with hunger in his eyes. *He must have done this before,* I thought just before I lost myself in his touch and his body.

The rest was a blur. A sweet mixture of pleasure and pain. I cried as he came inside me for the first time and he held me for a long time afterwards. I felt so many things that night: relief that it had all gone okay, sadness at my loss, heartbreak because it wasn't with Zahid and vulnerable to the point of feeling violated. Sarfraz held me and kissed my hair afterward.

"I don't deserve you," were the last words I heard before I drifted off to sleep.

Two weeks, one argument and seven love-making sessions later, I began to settle down to married life. I still thanked my lucky stars for giving me a husband like Sarfraz. I pushed all thoughts of Zahid away and concentrated on being the best wife I could. It didn't take much effort since I was beginning to genuinely care for Sarfraz. He was sweet and tender by day and deep and passionate by night. I once joked with him that he was probably an axe murderer because he seemed so perfect. He had just smiled with a mischievous glint in his eye before grabbing the kitchen knife and coming at me maniacally. My scream had caused his mother to come into the kitchen and she caught sight of what he was doing. She told him off playfully for constantly teasing me and he just laughed his sweet sexy laugh and winked at me. I felt so happy in that instant. His family had accepted me with open arms. I thanked Allah for keeping the balance - the same balance that had allowed me to do well academically to counter my family problems. I silently hoped it would last twenty years to counter the twenty years I had endured in my family home. I smiled as I thought, *ex-family home*.

"Come on lazy bones!" called Sarfraz to Sania who was lagging behind us.

"I'm tired!" she yelled.

"You're unfit!" he yelled back.

She made a grumbling sound in response.

Sarfraz laughed easily and turned his attention to me. "You okay, Kieran?"

I nodded as I walked along beside him on the grassy parkland path. He was wearing a light white shirt teamed with a pair of faded jeans and looked fresh and cool in the hot weather. I wore a cream *shalwar kameez* which billowed in the slight breeze. Since my wedding, I hadn't stepped into a pair of jeans or trousers. I knew that Sarfraz would not mind but I didn't feel comfortable wearing western clothes in his mother's house. It just didn't feel right.

"What are you thinking?" Sarfraz interrupted my thoughts.

"Nothing," I said.

He narrowed his eyes at me.

"I was just thinking about the past few months."

"What about them?"

I shook my head and he raised his eyebrows at me. "It's just that things have changed so much and I'm really happy. I know it's corny but… " I shrugged my shoulders.

"I love you too," he said, smiling. I stopped abruptly and looked up at him. He had his cheeky smile on and I wanted to hit him and kiss him all at the same time.

"Hm, you should be so lucky," I said.

"Oh, but I am," he replied, grinning.

"How much longer?" yelled Sania from behind us.

"Just around this corner," replied Sarfraz over his shoulder.

"It's sooo hot," she moaned as she approached us.

"There." He pointed.

I looked up and froze in shock. "No!" I said.

"Yep."

"No way!"

"Yes way," he said.

"Are you being serious?" I asked as we neared the gorgeous two-storey townhouse.

He nodded. "What do you think, San?"

"I like it," she replied, clearly impressed.

"Wait until you get inside," he said, as he unlocked the front door.

Sarfraz had received an offer from one of his estate agent friends. This beautiful property had just come on the market. It was in a beautiful location just off Wanstead Flats in a street straight out of a Rockwell painting.

"Oh my God!" I gasped as I walked into the huge living room. It was large and rectangular, with light beech wood floors and cool off-white walls. There were two large windows which flooded the room with the August sunshine. It was warm and spacious and I could already imagine the way it would look once it was furnished. We walked along the corridor into the kitchen. It was something straight out of a catalogue. I fell in love with it at once.

"How the hell can we afford this?" I turned to Sarfraz in wonder.

"So you want it?" he asked.

"Want it? I'd give my right arm for it!"

"Kieran! Come look at this!" yelled Sania from upstairs.

I ran upstairs to find her in the master bedroom which was beautiful. She pulled the curtains back to reveal a stunning view, overlooking the fields of Wanstead Flats, all green and lush in their summer prime. I gulped breathlessly and turned to Sarfraz.

"Are you kidding? We can't afford this place," I said.

"Don't you worry about it." He smiled warmly.

"What do you mean? We can't afford this place! Unless of course you're a part of some underworld Asian Mafia or something."

"Maybe I am," he said with a glint in his eye.

"Are you being serious? We can have this place?" I asked incredulously.

"Just say the word," he replied.

"YES!" I screamed and hugged him. He embraced me briefly and coughed, embarrassed in front of my little sister who was busy looking out over the balcony.

"This place is really cool. Imagine the kids running wild in that field. It'd be crazy," she called.

"Crazy," I said as I smiled up at Sarfraz.

September 6th 2003 - I had been married for just under three months. It had been a week since we had moved into our beautiful home and it was our first Saturday together. Sarfraz was working on some big account at work and had been stressed out by trying to juggle that with the move and leaving his mother. Leaving the family home was a big deal but Sarfraz knew that we would do it eventually so thought it better sooner rather than later. And though his family were great, I loved having our own space. Most girls in my situation would have to live with their in-laws for years, if not forever, so I counted myself very lucky. I had told him that we didn't have to move out immediately but he was fine about it, if a little tense at times. I had tried to convince him to take some time off but he insisted that it was impossible.

I wanted to make sure that he relaxed this weekend. I cooked him a nice meal (well, nice by my standards) and curled up with him on the sofa contentedly. The living room looked amazing now that it was finished. We had furnished it with white sofas and plump rich-coloured cushions, a long glass coffee table and a large luscious rug which covered nearly the whole room. It was my dream home and I hadn't worked for it at all. I still couldn't believe my luck. I sighed against his chest and flicked through the channels before settling on BBC2.

"The Weakest Link?" asked Sarfraz. "Is my little wife getting wise and boring in her old age?"

I play-punched him in the stomach. "No, I'm waiting for the Simpsons. It always comes on after this."

"Mm, I believe you," he said, smiling.

I narrowed my eyes at him and turned my attention to the program.

"What is the chemical symbol for Lead?" asked Anne Robinson, the host.

"Pb," I answered.

"I knew that," said Sarfraz.

"I bet you did," I said sarcastically.

"Oh, come on, what kind of loser do you think I am? Of course I knew that."

"Yeah riiight!" I laughed.

"Ok, come on then, competition," he said, turning to the television.

I was never one to back down from a challenge so I unwrapped myself from his arms and concentrated on the show.

"What P signifies a word that reads the same backwards as it does read correctly?"

"Palindrome!" I answered before Sarfraz had a chance. I laughed in delight as he threw me an evil look.

"Who is the US equivalent of Defense Secretary Geoff Hoon?"

"Donald Rumsfeld!" shouted Sarfraz.

"Pass," said the contestant.

"Donald Rumsfeld," said Anne Robinson with a look of scorn. Sarfraz whooped in delight.

"Okay, 2-1 to me," I said grudgingly.

"No! It's one-all," he replied.

"No! I got 'Lead' and 'Palindrome'."

"'Lead' wasn't a part of the competition."

"It was."

"It wasn't."

"Fine!" I replied. "One-all. Get ready sucker!" I turned my concentration back to Anne.

"What is the capital of Iceland?"

"Reykjavik!" yelled Sarfraz. "2-1 to me," he said with laughter in his voice.

I growled in response. We finished the program on 8-4 to Sarfraz and he looked at me teasingly.

"You think you're sooo clever, don't you?" I said.

"Well, I think that was just proven, don't you?" he said with a cheeky grin.

"I knew all the ones you did. You were just faster than me."

"I know sweetie, I know," he said, patting my arm in mock condescension.

"Just because you went to LSE." I poked him gently in the arm.

"Aw, my poor beautiful. Are you feeling inferior just because you went to a crappy university?"

I gasped with indignation. "How dare you? I did *not* go to a crappy university, Mister! At least we had social lives at Queen Mary unlike all you toffs at LSE!" I countered.

"Ah, as can be expected, ladies and gentlemen, to prevent her inferiority complex from becoming blatantly obvious to us all, she switches to attack mode. As we have witnessed on many previous occasions, offence is the best defence," he rambled to an imaginary audience.

"Okay, okay, enough!" I said holding up my hands in surrender.

He laughed that infectious laugh of his and looked at me triumphantly.

"You're right to some extent, you know that?" I said in the break before 'The Simpsons' started.

"About what?" he asked.

"The whole university thing. Don't get me wrong. I don't regret going to Queen Mary. I had a really fantastic time there but sometimes I think I could have done so much better."

"Hey, what are you talking about? You've done fantastically. I mean, what other Bengali girl do you know with a First Class degree from the University of London?"

"See, that's just the thing," I said. "It's always been 'Look at other Bengali girls'. I've always compared myself to other Bengali girls and the limits that applied to us. I was content with myself because I had done better than my peers but I never compared myself to anyone else. I never thought to reach any higher. When I was choosing universities, I didn't even *know* about LSE. My teachers deemed it wonderful that I had got into Queen Mary and it *was,* for a Bengali girl in Tower Hamlets, but sometimes I regret not doing more."

"Hey, if you feel that way, you can always go back to study. It *is* what you were planning to do."

"I know, but I'm not sure."

"Kieran, if it's something you want to do because you will enjoy it, then do it, but don't do it if it's just about proving your worth, because that's pointless. Tower Hamlets or not, you have come far and you should be genuinely proud of yourself."

I smiled at him. "Thank you for the wise words, Sensei. I will definitely think about it."

"Any time, Kieran-San."

The rest of the weekend flew by and before I knew it, Sarfraz was back in Stress Mode. One evening, he called to say he would be working late again. I promised him a warm bath and a decent meal when he got home. *Check me out on my Stepford Wife trip,* I thought as I replaced the receiver. Almost immediately the phone rang again. He had done this so many times. He would call me in the midst of doing something to tell me he would be late and then call me immediately after to apologise for being hasty or tense and to make sure that I was ok.

"I accept your apology on the condition that you bring me home a box of chocolates," I said, laughing.

"Kieran?"

I froze.

"Kieran?" asked the voice tentatively.

"Yes?" I said, almost choking on the word.

"Are you okay?"

"Zahid?" I whispered.

"Yes," he said, sounding relieved. It was hard to believe that it had been only three months since I had seen him last. It seemed like an eternity.

"How the hell did you get this number?" I asked shakily.

"It's not important. How are you?"

"What are you doing, calling my house, Zahid? What is this?" I was angrier at myself than him; angry because old feelings came rushing back with such force that I felt as if the wind had been knocked out of me.

"I just wanted to see how you are," he replied.

"Zahid, don't call here again. I am married now, okay?"

"I miss you," he said. And as simple as they were, those words bought tears to my eyes. It all came whirling back to me. The cold winter walks, the late evenings studying for our exams, countless meals at Nandos and Pizza Hut, warm Tunisian sunshine, laughing, kissing, touching. It all came back to me like some fucked up movie flashback.

"I miss you too," I replied before I could stop myself.

"Shit Kieran, you don't know how it feels to hear you say that. I thought I could just get on with my life. I thought I could just forget you but I can't. Kieran, I sound like a fucking wimp but I love you. I can't get over it. I can't forget you. This is so fucked up, Kieran. It's all fucked up."

I tried to shake my heart free of the feelings that were rushing back into it. "Zahid, I can't be doing this," I said.

"Wait!" he yelled desperately. "Just wait."

"For what?" I said angrily.

"Just give me a minute, Kieran. I've been going crazy without you. I've been yelling at my sisters and my mum. They think I'm on fucking drugs or something. I even yelled at my niece the other day."

I said nothing so he continued.

"Kieran, can we be friends?"

I almost laughed. "That's ridiculous and you know it."

"You don't understand. I need you in my life." He was interrupted by the text message alert on my mobile phone lying next to me. "Who's that?" he asked.

I checked the message. "It's my husband," I said, stressing the word 'husband'.

"What's he saying?"

"Nothing."

"Please tell me, Kieran."

"Why?"

"I just want to know what kind of guy he is."

"He's a good guy."

"Please read the message."

I sighed and re-opened the message. In a monotone I read it out: "My darling wonderful wife, I'm sorry for sounding short with you on the phone. What can I say? I'm a scoundrel, unworthy… " I paused as I opened the second message, "of your love. I tried to call back but the phone was engaged. Was gonna call your mobile at the risk of acting like a jealous husband but texted you instead. Be home soon."

Zahid said nothing. "Are you happy?" he asked after a long pause.

"Yes," I replied genuinely.

"Okay," he said but I could hear the quiver in his voice and it made my heart break.

"Kieran, I'm going to leave you alone now but I want you to know that I love you and if you ever need anything, you can call me. Okay?"

"Okay," I replied.

"Bye." He hung up.

"Goodbye," I whispered softly.

It was 11 p.m. by the time I heard Sarfraz's keys in the front door. I smoothed my light blue shalwar kameez, and greeted him at the door. "Are you okay?" I asked, noting that he wasn't his usual cheery self.

He nodded in response through bleary eyes.

"I'll fix up your plate," I said.

"No, it's okay. I ate," he said.

"You can't have eaten properly. I'll just warm it up." I walked towards the kitchen.

"Kieran, I ate," he repeated.

"Coffee and a donut right? You have to eat properly," I called over my shoulder.

"For fuck's sake, you're not my goddamned mother!" he yelled. The words stung like a slap. I froze in mid-step. I didn't know how to react. I knew he had had a long day and things probably weren't going well at work but his words still stung. "I'm having a shower. Just throw my food in the bin," he said coldly and stalked up the stairs. I turned and watched his back and bit back tears. I knew this was a one-off and that husbands were allowed a temper tantrum once in a while but I still felt hurt. I threw his food away just like he had demanded. I expected him to come back down any minute and apologise but he didn't. When I finally went upstairs, he was already in bed with his back turned to me. What had I done wrong? Did he somehow know that I had been talking to Zahid? But there was no way he could have known.

I willed myself to ask him what was wrong but thought the better of it. I quietly crept into bed and curled myself into a little ball. I could feel tears welling up in my eyes but I held them back. I knew I was lucky to have him and one temper tantrum in two months was hardly worth crying over but for the first time since my wedding night, I felt alone.

The next morning, I heard his footsteps approach the kitchen as I finished making a cup of coffee. It was weird because I knew I couldn't get angry at him. Anytime Zahid had yelled at me in the past, he had to practically beg for forgiveness but I knew I couldn't do that to Sarfraz because he was my husband and I had to respect him and be subservient to him. It didn't mean that women were inferior, just that we had to bite our tongues more often.

I turned to him and said, "Coffee?" I expected him to apologise, maybe even sweep me into his arms and ask for forgiveness but he simply shook his head. I stared at him for a second but he didn't seem to notice.

"Have you used up all the hot water?" he asked.

"No," I replied after a short pause.

"Okay, I'll be in the shower." He went back upstairs.

What was going on? He couldn't still be in a bad mood. Creeping doubt entered my mind. Was there some way he knew about Zahid? Why was he treating me so coldly? He was acting nothing like the Sarfraz I married. I read the morning paper whilst debating whether or not to confront him about his behaviour. I thought it best to leave it for now.

After a while, he came back down. He looked lovely in his suit and long coat.

"Sarfraz?" I said as he walked towards the front door.

"Yeah?" he called back.

"Um," I hesitated. "Have a nice day," I said.

"Thanks," he replied and walked out.

I sat there with my cold coffee and tried to figure out if I had done anything wrong. Apart from my conversation with Zahid, I had been the perfect wife. I put it down to the fact that he was missing his family and decided to show him the advantages of living alone with me.

I got ready and headed out to the West End. The journey was a bit longer than what I was used to but I loved living in Wanstead because it was quiet and peaceful, which was a sure sign that I was getting older. As I sat on the Central Line hurtling towards Oxford Circus, I smiled with thoughts of my task. It was Friday and I was going to give Sarfraz a night he wouldn't forget.

I browsed the shops for a couple of hours. I bought goodies from The Body Shop and La Senza then headed home to start getting things ready. I made a small pasta dish and then had a long bath. I exfoliated, shaved, moisturised and conditioned myself to perfection and hoped to God that Sarfraz wouldn't work late today. By the time I was finished at 6 p.m., I was the perfect mix of virginal innocence and an Ann Summers mannequin. Just as I checked myself a final time in the mirror, I heard the key in the door. YES! I thought as I shook my hair out. I heard him walk in and dump his briefcase on the floor. I heard him yawn and smiled to myself. I walked out and as sexily as I could, said, "Tired?"

His eyes widened as he laid them on me. His mouth opened in surprise at my sexy sheer camisole and knickers. I bit my darkened lips and looked at him suggestively. "What's this all about?" he asked, as he turned his back to me. Not the reaction I was hoping for but no matter. I walked towards him and helped him take his coat off.

"Keep going," I said, reaching for his tie.

He grabbed my hands and held them at his neck. "I can do it myself," he said. I didn't let that faze me. I breathed in, which pushed my breasts against the thin material. His eyes flickered toward them. "Kieran," he started but he was too late. I grabbed his shirt and pulled him towards me. I kissed him deeply and saw that he was as hard as a rock. I rubbed myself against his erection and let a moan escape my mouth. He responded by grabbing my shoulders and pushing me down onto the sofa. "Jesus," he said under his breath before climbing on top of me. "Oh, Jesus. What the fuck are you doing to me?" he asked, as he pushed himself between my legs. I moaned in response and began to undo his trousers. He left my camisole on but desperately took off my knickers. He pushed himself inside me and I gasped with pleasure.

He grabbed my shoulders and pushed as deep as he could. It felt so good, I thought I would go crazy. He ran his hands over me like he was about to lose me; like he had to get as much as he could before I disappeared. He kissed me hungrily.

"I can't help myself. You're too fucking sexy." He thrust inside me. After long, frenzied lovemaking I couldn't contain myself and screamed as he pushed deep inside. I grabbed his back and felt like I would faint from the sensation. It didn't take long for him to follow my climax and we both lay in an exhausted heap on the sofa. I stretched luxuriously underneath his heavy sexy body and breathed in his scent. *That ought to destroy the bad mood he's been in lately,* I thought but almost immediately after, he stood up and pulled his clothes on.

"I'm gonna go have a shower," he said and started to walk out the door.

"Sarfraz!" I said.

He turned towards me.

"Are you okay? Was that okay?" I asked.

"Yeah, it was nice," he replied and walked out. *Nice?* Despite the fact that I had just had the best orgasm of my life, I felt cold inside. What the hell was going on? One minute he's all over me and the next he can't wait to get away from me. I decided another bold move was in order. I crept upstairs and knocked on the bathroom door.

"Can I come in?" I called.

"I'm in the shower," he replied.

"I know," I said as I opened the door and walked in naked.

He turned and looked at me with a look of mild annoyance. "What do you need?" he asked, gesturing towards the toiletries cupboard.

I shook my head and grabbed a towel and quickly wrapped it around me. "No, nothing," I replied, hiding the hurt in my eyes as I walked out again. I sat on the edge of our bed. What the hell had happened last night to make him like this?

We spent the evening in cold silence. I double-checked that he didn't mind me going to Rayya's house the next day. I thought maybe that's why he was acting strange but he just nodded and said, "Yes, that's fine." I didn't question him further.

The next day, I entered Rayya's house to a flurry of shouts and screams.

"Kids!" I shouted. The shouting stopped and all at once, Rayya's four children came charging to the doorway. I hugged my eldest nephew and ruffled his hair. I gave the three girls a hug and kiss each. I squeezed them all tightly and laughed as they began to bicker again. I turned to Rayya and hugged her.

"Where's Sarfraz? Isn't he coming up?" asked Rayya.

"Oh no, like I said, he's got some stuff to do," I replied.

"You hungry? You betta be," said Rayya, as she led me into the kitchen. I greeted Jasmine, Shelly, Neha and Sania who were gathered in the kitchen, flicking through Rayya's old magazines.

"Mmmmmm," I said as I eyed the table already laid out with a feast. There was steaming white rice and hot curries and sauces.

"Grab a seat," said Rayya. "Isn't it nice to eat without any men around? We get to eat first for a change!" She grabbed my plate and heaped rice onto it. I opted for a gorgeous vegetable curry which I seasoned heavily with green chilli peppers and then sat down to a good hearty meal with my five sisters. It was nice being able to talk and laugh over a meal with good company. Sarfraz had been so distant - our last few meals together seemed like I was dining with a stranger.

"So how's the house? How's Sarfraz?" asked Jasmine as we finished up.

"Yeah, the house is still beautiful. I'm glad you guys liked it," I said, referring to their visit in the first week after we moved in.

"It's so gorgeous. You're so lucky," commented Shelly as she washed her plate. We finished our meal and retired to the living room. Rayya served tea and biscuits all round.

"So Kieran, you never mentioned Sarfraz. Is he getting along okay in the new place?" asked Rayya.

I was about to tell them that he was wonderful and perfect, etc, but decided to tell them the truth instead. "He's actually been acting kind of strangely," I said.

"Strange, how?" asked Jasmine.

"Nothing serious. He just came home from work on Thursday and was really moody and snapped at me and he's been like that since."

"What? Snapping at you?" asked Rayya.

"No, he's been fine, just a little cold," I replied.

My sisters laughed.

"It's called the Aftermath of the Honeymoon Period," said Jasmine.

"No, it's like he's changed. He was so sweet and these last two days, he's just really moody," I said.

"Trust me, he'll be fine," said Jasmine. "He's just getting used to everything."

"Yeah, I guess so," I replied and bit into my chocolate digestive.

Sania laughed and made a comment about how we were all old biddies now, married off and sitting around discussing our husbands over tea and biscuits. I had to laugh because if you had told me I would be in this situation a year ago, I wouldn't have believed it. I had grown up a lot since then. I was no longer a kid dancing around in Sania's room singing off-key on purpose. I no longer made silly bad jokes (Q. What did the lawyer call his daughter? A. Sue) or talked back-to-front to annoy people. I no longer worshipped Johnny Depp or swooned at the sight of Pharrell Williams. Wow, if this is Woman, maybe I didn't mind staying a Girl.

"Plus you have nothing to complain about." Shelly interrupted my thoughts. "Look at me: homeless, jobless, penniless and still trying to get my hubby over. You have none of that hassle."

"I don't even want to think about all of that," said Neha shaking her head sadly.

I supposed I *should* thank my lucky stars. Sarfraz *was* a catch and yes, he had been a bit moody lately but like Jasmine assured me, he would settle down and things would go back to normal.

We spent the rest of the day chatting easily until about 7 p.m. when my mobile rang. Sarfraz's name flashed up on screen.

"I'm downstairs," he said simply when I answered.

"Do you want to come up? Rayya said she'll make you a nice cup of tea?"

"No."

"Are you sure?"

"Yes."

"Okay, I'll be down in a few minutes," I replied sadly. I hung up and turned to my sisters. "He said he's really sorry but he's tired so maybe next time."

"Never mind," said Rayya. "But next time, you force him okay?"

I said goodbye to my sisters and nieces and nephews, left the flat and rode down in the lift alone. I spotted his car and walked over. As soon as I got in, he zoomed off.

"So how was your day?" I asked.

"Fine," he replied. I began to get really frustrated with him.

"Sarfraz, is something wrong?"

"Wrong?" he said, glancing at me quickly.

"Yeah, you just seem a little stressed lately."

"No, I'm fine. It's just work, Kieran."

"It's just that you've been a little distant these past few days."

"Like I said, it's just work."

"Are we okay with the mortgage? I mean, you don't talk to me about it. If we're in trouble I can get a job too. I've been meaning to anyway."

"No, the mortgage is fine. You don't have to worry about it."

I tried a little more but kept drawing a blank from him. I decided to give up in case he lost his temper with me again. We drove home in silence the rest of the way.

Things didn't improve over the next week. He didn't initiate conversation or lovemaking and was completely withdrawn. I began to seriously worry about him. I ran through the things that could be wrong. Crazy thoughts ran through my mind. Was he having an affair? I thought, but dismissed it just as soon as I had thought of it. There were no signs of infidelity. He had come home late a few times but I knew that his work was genuinely demanding. Also, wasn't it a well-known fact that men tend to be more attentive and loving towards their wives when having an affair? Sarfraz was being the complete opposite.

The second idea I had was even scarier. What if he was ill? What if there was something wrong that he wasn't telling me? I knew of people who developed serious illnesses but hid it from their families and became really withdrawn. Maybe that was it? The change in him was so dramatic that only something as serious as that could have caused it. I began to worry about it so much that I confronted him about it. He simply shrugged it off and denied acting strangely. I was beginning to get sick of his behaviour. The only other explanation was that he had somehow found out about my past with Zahid. I knew I had to talk to him properly about this because he was really making me feel like shit.

On a Friday night, after a near-silent meal, I couldn't take anymore.

"Tell me what's going on Sarfraz," I asked. He looked up sharply as if the sound of his name had hurt him. It was customary for a wife not to use her husband's name, as a sign of respect, but it had always been an easy exchange between us.

"With what?" he said.

"There's something wrong and I want to know what it is."

"What are you talking about?"

"You know what I'm talking about. I've tried to talk to you about it before but you keep avoiding the issue. Sarfraz, something has changed in you since a few weeks ago. What's going on?" I asked pleadingly.

"Kieran, you're being paranoid."

"I'm not being paranoid, Sarfraz. It's like you're a completely different person now," I insisted.

"Kieran, I have a headache," he said as he began to get up.

"No!" I yelled. "You're not going to do this. Not this time. There's something going on and I want to know what it is."

"There's nothing going on."

"There *is*."

"Kieran, I don't know what you're going on about."

"It's like you can't stand to be around me!" I yelled. "You're telling me you're the same guy you were on our wedding night? The same guy who made me those promises? You're telling me you're the same guy who first bought me to this house? Who made love to me for the first time? Are you that guy?" I was close to tears. I had put up with it for two weeks now and I hadn't realised how upset it had been making me.

"Kieran, calm down," he said coldly.

I bit my lip and looked at him pleadingly. "Sarfraz, whatever it is, you can tell me. I won't worry or get angry or cry but I can't take this anymore. You're making me feel like dirt, like an inconvenience in your life. I'm your *wife*. I deserve to know what's going on," I begged.

This finally got the reaction I wanted. His shoulders sagged and he breathed deeply in surrender and nodded. "Okay," he said.

I said nothing, afraid that he may change his mind.

"I think we should go to the living room." He beckoned towards the sofa. I sat next to him and he turned to me. "Okay," he repeated and bit his lip. I looked at him expectantly. "I was planning on telling you this in the first week of our marriage but then the issue went away for a while but it cropped up again a few weeks ago, and I should have told you about it right at the beginning but once I married you, I couldn't bring myself to ask you."

"Ask me what?"

"I… " he stopped. I silently urged him to continue.

"Kieran, I do care about you and I think I am very lucky to have you as my wife. I didn't suspect that I could care about you this much. When I met you, you seemed totally confident and sure of yourself but as I've got to know you better, I've seen this side of you I want to protect and love and… " his voice trailed off.

"Sarfraz, what are you trying to say?" I asked.

"I'm in love with somebody else," he said.

I froze. This was the last thing I was expecting. The room suddenly seemed darker. "What?"

He nodded and repeated it. I blinked and tried to think through the confusion. I couldn't help but feel hurt. I tried to remind myself that I, too, was in love with someone else. It didn't have to stop us from having a good marriage. "Okay," I said calmly. "An ex-girlfriend or something?"

He nodded in response.

"Okay," I repeated. We were silent for a while. "So you got upset that day because she contacted you again?" I asked, thinking that Zahid had done the exact same thing.

"Not quite," he replied.

I looked at him questioningly.

"She tried to break up with me."

"But… when? I mean, you've been acting strangely for a few weeks now. Before that… " I stopped. "You were seeing her before that?" I asked unbelievingly. He said nothing which of course, said it all. "You were seeing her before that?" I repeated.

He nodded.

"You've been having an affair? And you've been treating me like shit because she broke up with you?" I asked.

He looked at me right in the eyes. "We haven't broken up," he said.

The words slapped me in the face. "What are you talking about? You're still seeing her?" I felt more betrayed than I could imagine. Here's this guy that I've only known for a few months and he was killing me with his words.

"Kieran, I was going to tell you."

"But it slipped your mind?"

"No. I was trying to find the right time," he replied.

I stopped myself from screaming at him. "Sarfraz, you're my husband. We're married now. Don't you understand how wrong it is?" I said, controlling my voice.

"I know, Kieran. I debated it for months. We discussed it and we thought that maybe it could work."

"Work? What were you thinking? That you would just keep sleeping with her behind my back for how long? Forever?" I asked angrily.

"No, we were going to let you in on the deal," he said.

"What are you talking about?" I asked, feeling sick.

"Okay, I'm going to start from the beginning but you have to promise you'll hear me out," he asked earnestly.

I nodded, stupefied.

"This is exactly how it goes. Her name is Yasmin. I met her at university and we got together in our second year. We became really close but her parents are very strict so approaching them with a proposal for her hand in marriage was out of the question. When my parents started to bug me about marriage, we tried to break up but it was too hard. Kieran, she's like my right arm. I didn't know how to function without her so I thought about it for a while. I know it's stupid and crazy but I figured there's hundreds of girls in a similar situation - not wanting to get married but having to. I figured if I could get married to a girl like that, a girl who wants her own freedom and independence without scarring her family name, I could maybe," he hesitated, "make an arrangement where we both live our independent lives but as a couple. I meant to tell you straight away but I just couldn't find the words."

I said nothing. What could I say? It was the most ludicrous thing I had ever heard. I tried to get my thoughts in order and calm myself in order to articulate what I was feeling.

"Sarfraz," I started. I wanted to scream at him but I sat there and tried to control my anger and then tried again. "Sarfraz, you say you wanted a girl who didn't want the married life. How do you know that I don't?"

"Kieran, it was just the way you seemed: really smart and independent. You had your own plans. I could see that marriage was just a way of getting your parents off your back."

"But you didn't think to make sure? You thought you'd just play with me? You thought you'd play about with my life? This is my fucking *life* you're talking about!" I erupted. "What the hell were you thinking!? That you'd tell me to just fuck off and be your what? Your *roommate?* And you could carry on seeing this Yasmin? What the hell were you thinking?"

"It made sense at the time."

"Sense?" I screamed. "Sense! What are you talking about!? Sarfraz, I want a life. I'm not a fucking pawn in your fucking game. What the hell are you thinking? You can't just play about with people like this! I can't... So you *tricked* me into marrying you? What kind of person does something like this?"

"Kieran, just stop and think about it. Please. Just pause for a moment."

"I can't believe this. What are you doing?"

"Kieran, please, just listen to me. Please," he begged.

"No, I don't want to hear this."

"Kieran, did you want to marry me?" he said quietly.

I couldn't think straight.

"Kieran, answer me. When your parents bought up marriage, did you want to get married? Did you want to be a housewife and clean and cook and do the washing? Did you want flowers and chocolates and roses and the domestic bliss trip? Is that what you wanted?"

"No, but I -"

"Exactly. You told me yourself how you think it's sad that Asian girls can't move out on their own. This is what I'm giving you. A chance to do your own thing without the ties of marriage," he said calmly.

"It doesn't mean I *never* want to get married, Sarfraz. Don't I deserve someone to care about? To care for me?"

"You're free to, Kieran," he said. The words stung me.

"I'm your *wife,* Sarfraz. Your *wife.* Does that not mean anything to you? You just told me I can go fuck around with other men. Have you no respect for me at all? I'm not asking for your love. Just some respect!"

"Kieran, please. Just think about it rationally."

"And what about her? She's going to get married and what? You let her husband in on the 'deal'? You think he's gonna just let his wife fool around with another man? Some men have a little respect for their goddamned wives! What the fuck *is* this?" I screamed at him with my hands balled into tight fists. I got up and walked into the garden. I needed to breathe. I needed to clear my head. What the hell was happening? How could things unravel so fast? But there was no respite as Sarfraz followed me.

"I was going to tell you, Kieran, but you seemed so vulnerable after the night of our wedding and I couldn't bear to. And then we became close and… "

"I lost my virginity to you Sarfraz," I said as tears formed in my eyes "And it doesn't mean two shits to you. You couldn't give a fuck."

"No, it meant something Kieran, it did."

"What- An easy fuck? Was that what I was? Did you go and laugh with her about how lousy a lay I was? I was so scared Sarfraz!" I started to sob. "Do you know terrified I was that night? But you were so gentle and you know what? I thought, 'I could grow to love this man' and I was starting to, Sarfraz. I really was." The tears rolled down faster.

"I'm sorry, I should have told you," he said.

"No, you shouldn't have done it in the first place. Can't you see how wrong this is?"

"I know. I just- I didn't think you were the type to care."

"From what? A *two minute* conversation? You decided to base this sham of a marriage on a two minute conversation? You used me, Sarfraz. You came from her bed to mine. All those late nights and me acting like the stupid innocent wife at home doing the cooking and the goddamned cleaning. When were you going to tell me about this Grand Master Plan? How long did you want to use me for? How many fucks did I have to give out before you told me?" I asked bitterly.

"I was never meant to sleep with you."

"So I just happened to fall and land on your dick all those times?"

"Kieran, it wasn't supposed to happen like this. I was meant to tell you straight away but you were so… so fresh and beautiful, I couldn't help myself."

I didn't know whether to laugh or cry. "And she didn't mind you crawling between my bed and hers?"

"She didn't know," he said.

I shook my head in confusion.

"I told her that I had told you and that you were okay about it but then that one time you called me in the office, she was there and… "

"And?"

"And she's curious about you so when you called, she put you on speakerphone and you were telling me not to be too late because you had a special treat for me and she just put it together and I had to come clean."

"Let me guess, that was Thursday two weeks ago," I said recalling the night he had turned into this cold, hard stranger.

He nodded. "She made me promise not to sleep with you again and to tell you as soon as possible."

"That was two weeks ago. How many times have you fucked me since then?" I asked coldly.

He just shook his head. "I never meant for it to get into this mess. I thought I could provide you with what you needed- a home, security, a companion and you would be happy."

"So the first three months was all a farce? It was an act you put on to keep the Missus happy?"

"No, Kieran. I really enjoy your company and it was easy for me to be your husband. I like being with you. I just- I didn't know how to act with you after my argument with Yasmin. She's so important to me."

I hung my head in sadness. So this was what my 'balance' had delivered to me: a farce of a marriage and a cheat for a husband. I shivered in the cold and moved to go back inside.

"Kieran, talk to me about this. What are you going to do?"

"What am I going to do? What I *should* do is call this Yasmin of yours and tell her what is really going on. Tell her how you fucked me harder than you ever have just two days ago. I should slap you across the face for what you've done to me. You used me, Sarfraz. Wasn't she enough for you? You had to come home and fuck me too?"

"Kieran, I tried to stop you. Each time, I tried to stop it but… "

"But you just couldn't help yourself, right? I was just too hot for it, right? You just had to give me one?"

He shook his head and it pleased me a little to see shame in his eyes. "I'm sorry, Kieran. I am so SO sorry. I don't know what else to say."

"Well, neither do I. And Sarfraz, I really didn't deserve to be treated the way you've been treating me for the past three weeks. I've been worried sick about you, I haven't been eating properly. Do you know what it's been like for me?"

"Kieran, I'm sorry," he said again with pleading eyes.

I shook my head in disbelief and started to walk away.

"Kieran," he called. "What are you going to do?"

"Nothing, Sarfraz. I'm going to do nothing." And with that I went upstairs and crumpled onto the bed in a mixture of disbelief and sadness.

I had really thought it was going to work. I really thought Sarfraz was this amazing guy and I had been lucky. I had looked forward to building a life together and now it all lay in ruins. I remembered back to a conversation I once had with Zahid. He had joked that if I got married to someone else, he would carry on seeing me and persuade me to have an affair with him. Obviously, Sarfraz and this Yasmin had taken this idea one step further. This stuff was for movies and books and the occasional real-life feature in magazines. This kind of thing wasn't meant to be happening to me. I had had my fill of drama in life. I thought I could finally settle down with something real.

My practical self tried to soothe the betrayal I felt by telling me that maybe it wasn't such a bad set up after all. Indeed, many a girl out there would probably be happy to be in my shoes: a husband who provided for you but left you to do whatever you wanted. In reality however, it left me feeling so lonely. I thought I was going to share my life with him. I had given him my body and let him into my mind. I was prepared to give him everything and he goes and tells me I can fuck around with whoever I want. It made me feel sick and dirty and unwanted. I couldn't move. I didn't have the energy to think so I just closed my eyes and like so many times before in my life, just pushed all thought away and pretended like everything was fine.

The next morning I awoke to find Sarfraz sitting at the kitchen table with his head in his hands. "Good sleep?" I asked as I entered the kitchen.

He just stared at me forlornly.

"Kieran, I'm sorry," he said.

"I don't want to talk about it," I said.

"But we have to."

"Not right now, we don't."

"What are you thinking?"

"I'm thinking that I need a big breakfast in me." I opened the fridge. "We're almost out of milk."

"Kieran, please."

I turned to face him. "What Sarfraz? *What?*"

"Talk to me."

"I *am* talking to you."

"Tell me what you're thinking."

"So when do I get to meet this Yasmin character?"

He gulped and looked at me, clearly startled at the prospect of introducing the two women in his life to each other.

"Hey, if I'm going to lend her my husband on a permanent basis, I'd like to at least shake the girl's hand," I said easily.

"Kieran, are you okay? What's going on?" he asked.

"Nothing. I thought about your proposition and it makes sense. It suits me fine."

He looked at me in confusion. "But yesterday you were so upset."

"And I had reason to be, Sarfraz. You practically stole my life from me. I assume we're not having any children?" I asked with a challenging stare.

"I don't know, Kieran. Maybe we can work our way around it," he said.

"Sarfraz, you can't work your way around children. You have them or you don't. It's as simple as that."

"We can think about that later on in life. Explore other avenues," he said.

"And bring another poor soul into this colossal mess? I don't think so. So you continue reading the FT. I'm going to make coffee and go about being the perfect little wife that I'm meant to be."

"Kieran, you don't have to do anything for me. I mean cooking and cleaning wise."

"No Sarfraz, if we're going to pretend to be a couple, at least we can pretend right. In fact, while we're at it, let's lay down some ground rules." I pulled out a chair and sat opposite him with a pen and an envelope. "Kieran and Sarfraz's Rules of Marriage," I said, writing. "Number 1 - No fucking unless of course Sarfraz feels like it. Number 2 - No sleeping in the same room or being in a state of undress in front of each other unless of course Sarfraz feels like it. Number 3 - Honesty with each other at all times unless of course, Sarfraz has something to hide. Number 4 - No children. What would you like to add?"

He stared at me for a long moment and then finally said, "Nothing. I don't want to add anything."

"Okay, fantastic!" I slipped the envelope into a drawer and slammed it shut.

"Kieran, please. You're obviously not okay with this," he said as I headed towards the door with my coffee.

"I'm fine. Peachy keen," I called over my shoulder as I walked out of the room. I tried my best to keep from shaking as I began to sob silently. I walked up the stairs and locked myself in the bedroom. I cried for a long time and then lay on the bed staring at the ceiling for what seemed like hours. It's strange how you're never actually thinking when you're doing that. It had a numbing quality that had always worked to calm me. I heard Sarfraz's car outside as he headed off to work. I rolled over and curled myself into a tight ball. "Everything happens for a reason," I told myself over and over again.

Chapter 9. Pretences

"Your tie is wonky." I reached out to straighten Sarfraz's tie. He flinched as my finger brushed his neck and our eyes locked for a moment. It was the first time we had touched in a week. "We're going to be late," I said.

"Don't worry, these things always start late," he replied as he looked in the mirror checking his tie. He grabbed his keys and turned to me. "Ready?"

"As I'll ever be," I replied and followed him out the door.

It was our first public outing as a fake couple. It had been a week since our agreement and things were still awkward. Sarfraz had moved his things into another bedroom. We saw as little of each other as possible and had only eaten together once. I spent my days cleaning, cooking and shopping. He worked, came home and shut himself in his room until dinner at which time I had already finished my meal. I went to sleep every night feeling empty and lonely. *Is this my life now?* I questioned. I thought about going back to study. Now that Sarfraz was supporting me, I could afford to go back and study law like I had said in our first meeting. I occupied myself with thoughts of this. I didn't know where else to turn. My family was as big a mess as ever. Technically, now that my 'marriage' had unravelled, I was free to see Zahid and become involved with him again but after such a painful break-up, there was no way I could put myself in that situation again. And Zahid had a shot at a normal life. There were tons of eligible Pakistani girls out there and I was sure he would be happy with one, once he forgot about me. I thought about confiding in Rabika, one of my best friends, but thought better of it. Even though I trusted her with my life, this kind of thing always had a way of getting out, so I just kept quiet about it.

I got into the car and tried to relax. We were on our way to one of my cousin's weddings which meant all my family, both immediate and extended, would be there. It was so obvious that there was a rift between Sarfraz and I, I didn't know how we were going to hide it. We rode all the way in near silence. A little polite conversation to keep things civil was all that was exchanged. He put on the radio and 'Stand by Me' by Ben E. King was playing. It was one of my favourite songs but in that moment, I couldn't bear to listen to it. I sat squirming as it played out and wished the day was over.

When we got to the hall, I said a little prayer as I stepped out of the car. I wished to God that it would all go smoothly. Of course, I didn't have to worry at all. As soon as we stepped into the hall, Sarfraz changed into a completely different person, the one I thought I married. He was charming when greeting my relatives, engaging when talking to others and sweet and attentive towards me. He easily fielded questions about when we were going to have children and light-heartedly teased my sisters about being over-dressed. He seemed so easy and relaxed that I couldn't believe it myself. He caught me staring at him and winked at me; one that Rayya caught. Later on, she commented on how I was such a "lucky cow" to have a husband like him.

Various people came to greet us and commented on what a lovely couple we made. One particularly forward auntie pinched my arm conspiratorially. "If I had a husband as good looking as that, I'd already be… " She made a round gesture by her stomach indicating a pregnancy. I gave her an incredulous look and she burst out laughing. All my aunties around us also laughed at how embarrassed I was. Usually, this kind of thing was never discussed but I suppose everyone was in a jovial mood from the atmosphere of the wedding. I shook my head at them.

"There'll be none of that thank you," I commented.

"Silly girl. Before we know it, we will hear news of a *chotu* Kieran," she said, still laughing. I simply smiled and shook my head. *They'll never hear news of a little Kieran,* I thought to myself. I really didn't know how I felt about that. I didn't have any maternal instinct and had never really wanted children. My elder sisters had always insisted that that would change; that once you get to a certain age, maternal instinct kicks in and that I would definitely want to have children when I was older. Maybe twenty-two was a bit early for it to have kicked in but I doubted it ever would. My relationship with my own mother had erased any desire to have children of my own, to create another mother-child bond. *Maybe Sarfraz really has struck lucky with me,* I thought bitterly.

I excused myself from the band of ladies and tried to relax. I felt so tense and seeing Sarfraz the way he used to be just made me really really sad. This is who I could be with but instead he saved all his charm and wit for Yasmin and the public. When we were alone, we were like business partners, cold and emotionless. I yearned for the warmth and laughter he was radiating.

I remembered that Zahid once told me that I loved being the victim; that because I had grown up amid chaos, it was the only thing I felt comfortable with and that if ever I was happy and balanced, I did something to screw it up. I began to think his words were true because as I watched Sarfraz chat easily with my cousins, a little piece of my heart gave into him. I felt it stir and yearn for him and everything he stood for and it made my eyes tear up. I lowered my head and concentrated on the plateful of rice in front of me. I took a drink of water and swallowed my sadness.

The next day Sarfraz came home with a big smile on his face.

"You look happy," I commented casually.

"I am!" he exclaimed. "Guess what?"

"What?" I asked.

"I made partner!"

"You're kidding," I replied as a smile grew on my face in reaction to his delight.

"Yes, they told me today!" he yelled excitedly.

"Oh my God, that's fantastic!" I yelled too, catching his enthusiasm.

"Yep! We're going out to celebrate!" he said happily.

"Really? Where?" I asked, surprised.

"Well, there's this Italian place near my workplace called Tassili's that I really love so we're going there."

"Sounds good." I mentally wracked my brain for something nice to wear.

"Yeah, it should be," he said. "Yasmin is still getting ready so I'm gonna go pick her up in about half an hour. I've been waiting for this for years and to finally get here is the best feeling in the world!" he said happily.

"Oh. That's really brilliant." I hid the hurt in my voice.

"Yeah, you should have seen the way they told me. They just completely sprung it on me. I walked in thinking it was a normal meeting. They had kept it all under wraps. Usually, they advertise internally but this time, for some reason, they awarded it to me," he yammered excitedly.

"You should be proud of yourself," I said genuinely. I wasn't able to hide the tinge of sadness in my voice.

"Hey," he paused, "you gonna be okay?" he asked with the first hint of concern I had heard in a long time.

"I'm -" I was cut short by his mobile ringing.

He answered it quickly. "Hello? Yeah, I'm ready. Now? Sure, okay, see you in a bit. Okay, bye," he hung up. He looked at me to see my reaction. It was the first time he had spoken to Yasmin in my presence. I simply acted nonchalant so he picked up his coat and headed out.

"I'll see you later, Kieran," he called over his shoulder.

"Yeah, bye," I called back, disguising the pain in my voice.

How did I get into this situation? My husband was going to dinner with another woman. I couldn't help but imagine him laughing and touching her, getting close to her and making intense love to her like he did to me during the first few months of our marriage. My heart ached at the thought and more than ever, I wanted to go to Zahid and fall into his arms and succumb to him. I shook the thought out of my head. It had been just under four months that I had been married and I had started to get cabin fever. I needed something; whether it was a job or study or just a hobby. I couldn't stay cooped up like this at home forever. I decided that I would start job-hunting the next day.

On exactly the fourth month 'anniversary' of our wedding, I was offered a job at the Greenwood Institute of Preventive Medicine as an IT Analyst. It was a medical research centre based in Barbican and I was to join the small IT team as an all rounder - graphics work, user support, web and database development, etc. The pay was twenty-three thousand pounds per year, which was peanuts compared to what Sarfraz earned but I knew I had to do something to keep myself from going crazy. Things with Sarfraz had not got any better. I thought that after his display of delight the night of his promotion, he would start being more open with me but he was clearly adhering to Yasmin's rules.

Work provided a distraction and I poured my energy into it. Getting out of the house helped to clear away the cobwebs that had began to form in my mind. I had always been mentally active but had done no challenging work since my degree had finished, so I looked forward to starting my job. The first week went by in a whirlwind of orientation, health and safety talks and introductions. I shared an office with a database developer who was quiet but pleasant. It wasn't long before I settled in and started to enjoy myself.

The Friday after my first week of work, I was both exhausted and happy. I got home to find Sarfraz sitting on the living room sofa. I approached him as he read the evening paper. He glanced up, nodded and went back to his paper.

I sat on the sofa opposite him. "Why don't we talk?" I said.

He looked up. "What do you mean?"

"I mean, we live together right? And yes, we're husband and wife but we're not really, obviously. And I know we're civil to each other but what is stopping us from being more?"

He shook his head in confusion.

"More as in friends I mean. Do we have to act like strangers to each other? You're in love with Yasmin and of course she can't be happy with you living with another woman but you're obviously not interested in me so what's stopping us from being friends and a bit more open with each other?" I asked, verbalising the feelings that had been dwelling in me for weeks.

Sarfraz set down his paper. "That's just the thing Kieran. You say I'm not interested in you but I *am* interested in you."

I said nothing so he continued.

"I *am* in love with Yasmin but that doesn't stop me from caring about you. Those first few months with you, I felt like I was… I felt the way I felt when I first met Yasmin. I felt like you were someone I could have fallen in love with in another time and another place. Kieran, you're smart and sweet and beautiful. For God's sake, I couldn't stop myself from sleeping with you even though I knew I wasn't meant to. *That's* what you do to me when I get close to you, so the only way for me to deal with it is to not get close to you."

I didn't really know what to say to him. "So, I'm being punished because you're in love with someone else and I'm being punished because you 'could' fall in love with me?" I asked. "That doesn't make sense, Sarfraz. If I'm someone you could care about then why don't you? Why don't you leave Yasmin? Why don't you give us a shot?"

"You know I can't," he replied.

"Why not? I'm your wife, Sarfraz. If you know you could love me, then why not try? Why live this double life, always sneaking around, lying to our friends and family? Why sacrifice children and a decent future for us?"

"Kieran, I can't listen to this."

"Sarfraz! You have to listen to me ok? I am your *wife!* You may treat me like a complete stranger but you can't deny that. Do you think what you're doing is forgivable? Do you think it's *Islamic?* The Quran states that you are responsible for taking care of your wife."

"I *am* taking care of you!" he yelled back.

"So that excuses everything does it? Don't you get it? You're being unfaithful! You may not see this as a marriage but by Islamic law, we *are* married and every time you sleep with her, you're making things worse for yourself! How can you even call yourself a Muslim?" I shouted.

"Oh, don't you bring religion into this!"

"Well, what else is there? You obviously don't care for morality or honesty or common decency! Can't you see how wrong this is?"

"Where is all this coming from, Kieran? You were fine about it and now, all of a sudden, you're going crazy on me. What's going on?"

"I want a divorce," I said falteringly.

"I'm not listening to this," he replied as he grabbed his car keys.

"Sarfraz, stop walking away from me. I'm your fucking wife! Listen to me!" I screamed but he just carried on walking. I ran after him but he slammed the door shut just as I got to him. I pounded the door and screamed in frustration.

"What the hell am I meant to do?" I screamed at him through the door. "WHAT!?" I slid down to the floor and sobbed like I had so many times in my family home. *Nothing has changed.*

That Sunday, Sarfraz and I were due to attend Shelly's wedding reception. Her husband, Shahin, had been allowed entry into the country and my sisters were holding a little party for them. This would give everyone who had not attended the wedding a chance to meet her husband and bless the happy couple. By then, I had got used to the idea that she had married Shahin. I had changed my opinion of him being a creep because I saw that Shelly was happy. She seemed genuinely happy but a part of me couldn't help but think that she had agreed as a way of making our parents proud of her. I knew that deep down, a part of her always looked for their approval. My mother had disapproved of us all our lives and maybe Shelly thought that this was her chance of finally being accepted and praised. I had given up hoping for my mother's approval a long time ago. I just hoped that Shahin would make Shelly happy. As for the part about them being first cousins, there was nothing I could do about that so I just ignored it. Most Bengali people did not see that to be an issue at all so it was easy to forget.

I had not spoken to Sarfraz since our argument but I had to approach him on Saturday night. "Are you still okay for Shelly's thing tomorrow?"

"Yes," he replied.

I hovered there for a second, wondering if I should say anything further or bring up our argument. Half of me regretted bringing up divorce but the other half told me that I was right in doing so. Mentioning divorce to one's husband was the greatest disrespect you could show him and in our culture, a wife's respect for her husband was the most important thing in marriage. Ours was hardly a conventional marriage so I forgave myself for saying what I had. "I'll wake you up at ten," I said.

"Okay," he replied.

The next day, we both got ready in silence. I was more nervous than I had been the time we had attended my cousin's wedding. Things were awkward then but now they were just sour. The tension between us was palpable and no matter how good Sarfraz's acting was, there was no way on earth he could make things seem right.

Of course, my predictions were proven wrong. Sarfraz slipped into Charm Mode as soon as we were in public. I shook my head at him, this time in disgust rather than wonder. *He had fooled me so easily,* I thought. Despite the fact that he had been in love with Yasmin, I had believed that my first few months with Sarfraz were genuine, with genuine emotion, genuine conversation and genuine experiences. Now I knew that this great, funny, sweet guy was all an act. He turned it on and off as if it was on tap. I didn't want to play role in his façade so I left him chatting to one of my uncles and went off to find my sisters.

I found them in a group chatting to my cousins.

"Have you found a place yet?" asked one of my cousins.

"No, I'm looking though," replied Shelly.

"So you're gonna be living at your mum's?"

"Yeah, in the meantime."

"Are you on the waiting list?" asked my cousin, referring to the local council's waiting list of people requiring accommodation.

"No."

"Why not?"

"Well, I'm going to apply now. I didn't want to before because I didn't want to jeopardise my husband's chances of getting his visa but now that he's here, I'm going to apply."

"If you go homeless, they'll find you a place," said my cousin.

"But it'll be a temporary place," replied Shelly.

"Yeah, but eventually they'll give you a permanent place."

"But I'm low priority," said Shelly.

"So get pregnant, girl!" said my cousin laughing.

I said nothing but simply shook my head. I found it sad that Bengali girls settled for so little - a husband from Bangladesh who could not really support them, a life's worth of income support and a council property for which the rent was paid by housing benefit. They were happy with this simple life and rarely aimed for anything higher. I knew that Shelly wanted to go back to university whilst her husband supported her but I didn't know how realistic that was. They were either going to have to live off income support or she would have to work since his income alone (when he got one) would definitely not be enough to support them. *At least she's happy,* I thought to myself as I watched Sarfraz at the other end of the room. *Which is more than I can say for myself.*

Another week flew by. I settled in at work and was really enjoying myself. I worked as part of an IT team supporting a group of medical researchers. I worked directly under a professor who was well-known in his field for a various number of activities. He tried his best to get me involved in the medical aspects of my work and took an interest in both my professional and personal life. During one particular meeting when discussing medical screening, he commented that having children helped reduce the risk of breast cancer in women.

"Are you planning to have children soon?" he asked me.

I was rather taken aback by the question. "I am but I would like to wait a while longer," I replied.

"Well, you are twenty-three, are you not?"

"Twenty-two."

"Yes, twenty two. You know, you are at the perfect age for breeding."

I simply nodded my head.

"What about your husband? Is he not keen?" he asked.

I cleared my throat and looked around for some way to change the subject. "He is, yes, but we're still finding our feet. Maybe in a few years," I said.

"Well, you don't want to wait too long. Women these days get caught up in their careers and start to have children later. That's when complications can occur. From my experience, Asian people tend to have their children young, which is good. Did your parents start having children fairly young? I assume they did."

"Yes. They did." I nodded.

"So you have no immediate plans?"

I shook my head, hoping he would change the subject. I was never maternal; never the type to bend over buggies and coo at passing babies but it didn't mean that I didn't want children one day. I thought back to my argument with Sarfraz. He had said that we would 'work our way around it'. I shook my head sadly at the memory.

"Either way, good luck," said the professor.

"Thank you," I replied.

On my way out, the professor's secretary, Andrea, stopped me.

"Ah, don't listen to him. Trust me, I had my one when I was thirty-three and I'm glad I waited. Any younger and I could not have handled the demon child."

I nodded.

"You okay? You seem a bit pale," said Andrea.

"I'm fine," I replied, waving away her concern.

Work gave me respite from the constant chill I felt at home but after a few months, I began to crave more. They say the grass is always greener on the other side and I began to see that was definitely true. When I had been 'only' a housewife, I'd wanted to work and be occupied but now that I was working, I was growing tired of it. It was not so much my work but the journey that was taking it out of me. Getting on the crowded Central Line every morning was such a nightmare. I know all journeys in London are a nightmare between eight and nine in the morning but the Central Line was like a sauna.

Obviously, having been born and bred in London, I knew how bad the trains could get but I had never had to travel on the Underground on a daily basis before and certainly not during rush hour. All my schools and even my university had been within walking distance of my family home so this was the first time I truly experienced the rat-race.

I hated how petty it all was. I hated the little pang of triumph I felt when the train doors stopped directly in front of me. I hated the way people pushed and shoved to get on carriages and escalators first. Manners went out the window. The London Underground was a free-for-all and I hated the way people treated each other. I hated the way people took up a quarter of the space on my seat. I am a small person: 5 feet 1 inch tall, weighing 7 stones. I think I'm a lightning rod for overweight, obese and generally broad shouldered people. They see me and think, *"Ah, there's a girl that doesn't need all that extra space, I'll go sit next to her so I can spread myself out."* I know that is not incredibly polite or politically correct but as I said, common decency and manners are suspended as soon as people enter an Underground station.

I hated the way people with huge backpacks seemed to forget that they were carrying them and swung around and knocked into everyone standing in a one-metre radius of their backside. I hated people who held their large umbrellas horizontally which meant you had to walk at least five steps behind them to avoid having your legs skewered. I hated people who leaned on the poles on the train so that no one else could hold onto them. The London Underground really bought out the worst in people and experiencing it for two hours everyday was really beginning to get to me.

If Sarfraz and I had been a real couple, I would have considered giving up work and dedicated myself to him and maybe started a family. In fact, I probably would not have started to work in the first place. I kept telling myself that I was lucky because I was free to be my own person. I knew girls who got married and were living with their in-laws who directed every part of their lives. When I was living at home I had always craved freedom. Now I was free to do whatever the hell I wanted and yet I was still unhappy.

I often watched Sarfraz come home so obviously satisfied from a session with the illustrious Yasmin. He had shown me her picture a few weeks ago after much persuasion. She was pretty, not the beautiful heavenly creature I had imagined but pretty nonetheless. I had stared at her for the few minutes he had allowed me before snatching the picture back and gruffly proclaiming, "That's enough." I scolded myself for getting jealous. I mean, if anything, she had a right to him more than I did. She had known him for four years now. In comparison, I was a complete stranger to him but something inside me was deeply saddened by the fact that I wasn't enough for him. Was I ever going to be enough?

Chapter 10. Ravaged

It was Sunday morning and our six-month anniversary. I know it's stupid to count the days but I still noted it for posterity. Sarfraz had nothing planned and I yearned to ask him to go out with me. Just for a meal or a movie or a normal activity that normal platonic friends could do but I didn't. Instead, I decided to have a nice long bath and spend the day with a good book. I took my time in the bath and luxuriously indulged myself, something that I really needed to do. Work was okay but it had really begun to suck all the energy out of me. I lazed for an hour before finally getting out. I reached for my bathrobe and realised that I hadn't bought it in with me. I wrapped my hair towel round my body instead and stepped out onto the landing.

As I turned the corner to enter my bedroom, I nearly crashed into Sarfraz. I almost dropped my towel from the scare.

"Jeez Sarfraz, you scared the living daylights out of me."

"I'm - I'm sorry," he said quickly.

I shook my head. "It's fine." I waited for him to get out of my way but he simply stood there staring at me. His eyes trailed down to my chest and then travelled down my body. I suddenly realised that the tiny towel barely covered my buttocks and was fit to burst against my breasts. I was wet, glistening and fresh out of a shower. I bristled under his stare and took a tiny step back. He did nothing to hide the lust in his eyes.

"Excuse me," I said as I brushed past him into my bedroom. I quickly shut the door and dressed. A part of me felt angry because he had no right to look at me like that but another tiny part of me was secretly pleased. He wanted me and it was good to know.

I cooked us a simple lunch which I ate in the kitchen and he in the living room. We watched some TV together and I did some grocery shopping. I lazed about for the rest of the day and then finally retired to bed. I wrapped the blankets tightly around me to keep out the December chill and slowly drifted off to a gentle sleep.

It was 2 a.m. when I was woken by the sound of my bedroom door being cracked open. I sat up and watched a silhouette enter my room. For a split second I froze in fear as I thought it was a burglar but then realised it was Sarfraz. I blinked sleepily and rubbed my eyes.

"Sarfraz, what's going on?" I asked.

"Sssh," he said as he came closer.

"Is everything okay?"

"Mm," he said as he climbed onto my bed and looked at me. I could see something dark in his eyes, anger or… lust. "Kieran," he mumbled as he reached for me.

"Sarfraz, what is this?"

"Kieran," he repeated as he held my shoulders and kissed me.

I recoiled and jerked away from him. "What the hell do you think you're doing?"

"Ssh." He pushed me down onto the bed.

"Sarfraz, what are you doing? Stop it," I said as he climbed on top of me and began to kiss me. I could feel his hard-on press against my stomach and realised how much I had missed the feeling. I breathed in his manly scent as he kissed me. "Sarfraz, stop," I said half-heartedly.

"Kieran, I want you. I want you so fucking bad. You're driving me crazy. I'm going crazy. Watching you every day, being near you and not being able to touch you. I can't do it. I can't do it," he said in-between kisses.

I resisted his lips for long enough to say, "You can't have it both ways, Sarfraz. You have to choose. You can't have me as well as her." I tried to push him away.

"I want you," he moaned as he lifted my nightgown. "Only you." He slipped his fingers underneath the band of my knickers. It had been so long since I had felt a man's hands there. "I can't stop thinking about you," he moaned. "How you feel, how you taste. I want you so bad. I haven't been able to get rid of this hard-on since seeing you this morning. Kieran, I tried. I tried to stop myself but I want you so bad."

I struggled a little against his weight. "I don't want to do this," I said, clearly being contradicted by the moisture between my legs. "Sarfraz, you can't have me too. I'm not going to be second best." I tried to sit up.

He grabbed my wrists and held me down. "You're not, Kieran. I only want you. I'll break up with Yasmin. Whatever you want, just let me please. Please," he begged, almost frenzied.

"No Sarfraz, you can't make a decision like that now." I was still trying to push him off.

"I can. I am. I just want you." He slipped a finger inside me. I moaned in pleasure. I couldn't say no to him. How could I say no? He undressed me quickly and rubbed himself against me before finally pushing his way inside. I succumbed to him completely and it was the most heavenly feeling in the world. I sat up and gripped his shoulders allowing him to thrust inside me as hard as he wanted. His sweaty sexy body slammed into mine as he thrust into me as hard as he could. I screamed in abandon as we did it faster and harder. It was the most liberating experience I had ever had. He wanted me desperately and it was the greatest feeling in the world. *If only Yasmin could see us now,* I thought just as I felt the build-up inside me.

"I'm gonna come!" I screamed as he grabbed me and ground himself into me. "Oh Jesus, Oh Christ! Oh fuck!" I screamed as the sensation ripped through me. My muscles contracted around him which only made him go faster. He continued until he too came to a crashing climax. I couldn't believe how amazing it all felt. I felt high and dizzy and relaxed all at the same time. I breathed in his smell and the warmth that was created between our bodies. It was the most amazing feeling in the world and I lay there enjoying it for a few minutes.

After a while, I turned to face Sarfraz expecting him to be falling asleep slowly. Instead, I found him staring up at the ceiling with empty eyes. Fear struck at my heart.

"Sarfraz?" I asked. He turned to me and the regret was clear in his eyes. *No,* I thought. He wasn't going to do this to me. Not again. He's not going to fuck me and discard me again. No way. "What's the matter?" I asked, already feeling sick to the stomach.

"I'm going back to bed," he said. I looked at him wildly.

"Why?" I asked.

"Because I want to," he replied.

"But - " I started.

"I'm tired, Kieran. We'll talk about this in the morning." He reached for his boxers.

"Wait, what just happened?"

"We had sex," he replied simply.

"Sarfraz, what are you doing? Why are you being like this? You said that you… " my voice trailed off.

"Kieran, we'll talk about it in the morning," he said.

"Wait!" I cried, grabbing his arm. "You're telling me that was just a fuck? Is that all it was?"

He said nothing.

"No, Sarfraz. You want me," I said desperately. "Come, let's do it again. Come on. I want to," I said touching his chest. "You think you can handle it again?" I asked, kissing his chest desperately.

"Kieran, stop it," he said coldly.

Oh no, I wasn't going to let him get away with this. I wasn't going to let him leave me like this. He wanted me. *I'll make him want me again.* "Oh, you don't want to play?" I asked, rubbing my breasts against his chest. "I'll be good. I promise. I'll even… " I paused and looked down at his boxers with my tongue between my teeth.

He shook his head and began to walk out.

"Sarfraz, come on. I know you want to. I don't mind. Let's do it again. I want to do it again." I threw my arms around him.

"Kieran, stop it," he said impatiently.

"Oh, so you only wanna play when it suits you? Well, I want to NOW," I said and fell to my knees. I pressed my mouth against him and felt him grow hard again. I looked up at him seductively. "Now that's more like it." I kissed him through his boxers harder. He let me carry on for a minute before taking a step back. I could see the strain in his eyes.

"Kieran, get up," he said.

"No," I said reaching for him. He hooked me through my arms and lifted me up. "No!" I yelled as I went for him again. I pushed my body against him and rubbed myself against his erection.

"Kieran, stop it," he said. "Stop it," but I continued. "Stop it!" he screamed and then lifted me by my arms and threw me onto the bed. "Stay the fuck away from me!" He stalked out of my room, slamming the door behind him.

I couldn't breathe. I couldn't cry, I couldn't think for the pain. It rushed at me all at once and winded me with its force. My face crumpled. I opened my mouth but the sobs caught in my throat. After a few seconds, they came crashing out and wracked through my whole body. I lay there naked, bruised, rejected and destroyed.

The next day, the only sign of Sarfraz was the front door slamming at seven in the morning when he left for work. I was glad he was gone because I did not want to face him. I was ashamed and angry with myself. I was disgusted at the way I had acted last night. I had never behaved so desperately. Something just broke inside me after he had got up to leave. He had treated me like a rag doll: picked it up to play with and then thrown it down once he was finished.

I had just wanted to feel wanted again. When he'd come into my room last night, I had felt like I was the only woman in the world. The way he had looked at me with deep desire had made me feel special and wanted. I had always despised weak women and had always thought of myself as strong and independent. Now I knew that that was all an illusion and I was just as needy as any woman out there. I had needed to feel something last night; something other than rejection and pain but by pushing myself onto him, that's exactly what I had got.

I ached both in body and in mind. I was still shaken by his burst of violence when he threw me onto the bed. It had knocked the wind out of me. I knew he was tortured. He loved Yasmin but he found living in close proximity with me difficult. But if he wasn't even going to address me as something other than a complete stranger, what right did he have to my body? I was angry with him but angrier with myself. I had given into him so easily. For months he had ignored me and treated me like crap and as soon as he got a hard-on, I was all over it. I felt like throwing up but instead, I dressed quickly and crept out of the house.

I tried to breathe in some fresh air to calm myself but felt it scratch at my throat instead. *Levolle? Levon? No, it was longer than that... Levonelle!* Levonelle was what I was after. I had seen an advertisement for it on the Underground. "If you don't want the whole world to know that you're after the morning-after pill, ask for Levonelle," it had said.

I had stopped taking contraceptive pills the day Sarfraz had told me about Yasmin. Yesterday, neither of us had had the presence of mind to find a condom so here I was, in a situation I never thought I would find myself in.

I pulled my coat tight around my body and quickened my pace. I didn't really have any qualms about taking the morning-after pill. I did not think about the fact that there could be a life growing inside of me nor about the fact that taking the pill was un-Islamic. I just wanted to make sure that my weakness would not lead to more heartache. I walked into the chemist and breathed a quiet sigh of relief that the pharmacist behind the counter was white. I could not bear to ask an Asian man for it.

I cleared my throat as I walked to the counter. He was a tall man with grey hair and thin framed glasses.

"I'm looking for some Levonelle," I said.

"Levonelle?"

"Yes," I replied nervously. I hoped to God he knew what I was talking about.

"Please wait one minute," he said as he headed to the back. I tried not to look at the woman behind the counter and concentrated on the perfume aisle instead. A few minutes passed and the man finally returned with a small purple box in his hand.

"Have you taken emergency contraception before?" he asked.

I shook my head.

He took me to one side and asked a series of questions about my menstrual cycle and when I had had unprotected sex. I answered his questions quickly and concisely. He told me to make sure I read the instruction booklet and handed me the box with a sympathetic smile.

"Thank you," I said as I took it from him. I paid and left hurriedly. I tried to shake off the embarrassment I felt. *Grow up,* I told myself. *Girls do this all the time!*

I walked home quickly and sat down with the instructions. I know it's sort of morbid but I wanted to know how it worked. The pharmacist had told me that it would only work if I was not pregnant already. It did not work as an 'abortificant', the booklet said; the pill did not terminate a pregnancy. It simply prevented a fertilised egg from attaching itself to the womb. I felt queasy and quickly moved on to the statistics. 95% effective within 24 hours of unprotected sex, 85% between 25 to 48 hours and 58% if taken between 49 to 72 hours. Therefore it was 95% certain to prevent me becoming pregnant. I nodded nervously and walked to the kitchen counter. I was probably making it a big deal for no reason. I knew girls, *unmarried Muslim* girls, who had taken the morning-after pill on more than one occasion. I popped out the single pill and poured myself a glass of water. I said a little prayer despite the fact that taking the pill was against my religion and swallowed it quickly with a gulp of water. I drained the rest of the glass and resolutely placed it down on the counter. There was no way I was bringing a child into this godforsaken house.

The next time I saw Sarfraz was Monday evening after work. He walked in the door and our eyes locked. I looked away immediately but he walked towards me.

"Kieran, we need to talk," he said.

I said nothing. I was tired of it. I was tired of him and this situation. I wanted to get out. I felt trapped just like I had felt trapped in my family home. I felt like I was suffocating.

"I want to say sorry for what I did to you on Saturday. I've been beating myself up about it ever since. What I did was out of line. All of it. I used you and I shouldn't have. I know you tried to stop me but I wanted to… I wasn't thinking straight and I know I made you stupid promises but I think we both know that I wasn't in any state to be making promises."

I said nothing.

"And what I did to you after, I… " he stopped and looked down in despair. A wisp of hair curled over his forehead. In another lifetime, I would have found it endearing and perhaps brushed it away but now, I just stared at it rather than into his eyes. "I think I'm going mad, Kieran. Yasmin is driving me crazy with her jealousy and you… " he paused, "I hate the way you look at me. I see it in your eyes, Kieran. I swore to myself before I married you that I would give you everything you needed but now I know that I haven't and I can't. I see the sadness in your eyes. There was light and life in those eyes, Kieran. There was fight and zest and I may well have killed all of that. I know it's my fault and I hate myself for what I've done to you." I could hear the emotion in his voice. His words bought tears rolling from my eyes.

I looked up at him. "Then stop," I pleaded. "Stop it, Sarfraz, because I can't do this anymore."

"Kieran, anything. I'll do anything but I can't do that. Yasmin needs me more than you do. She's had a tough life and I love her and I've tried to break it off with her but I can't manage it. I was hoping you could get used to it but I've seen what it's doing to you and I'm stuck."

"Sarfraz, please. Don't you see? You are going to have to break it off with her sooner or later. What happens when she gets married? You will have to stop seeing her and all this will have been for nothing. This is killing me. I'm begging you," I said, releasing every last piece of dignity I had retained. I never thought I would be in this kind of situation. I always thought that if a man cheated on me, he would be out the door. No second chances, no recriminations, just a clean cut goodbye. In reality, it was so different. I was willing to accept everything he had put me through if only he agreed to give her up.

"Kieran, it's not as black and white as that. I know you can't understand but I can't leave her. I know it's killing you but I'm lost. I don't know what to do."

I wanted to shout at him. I wanted to tell him that I *could* understand. That I, too, was in love but had given it up to be with him but the words got stuck in my throat. Instead, I simply said, "Don't do anything. I know when I've lost." I stood up and walked out.

The next day, I woke to find a missed call on my mobile phone from Zahid. My heart leapt at the sight of his name. I missed him so much. I missed his voice and his face and his touch. I missed everything about him. I wanted so much to speak to him but I knew that would only dredge up feelings I had tried so hard to forget. I couldn't believe that I had walked away from him and walked into this nightmare instead. Life would be so much better if I had been brave enough to stand up to my parents. Instead, I had allowed them to assimilate me into the worldwide group of perfect Asian wives. Despite how determined, ambitious or independent a young Asian girl is, she always gives in to her parents' wishes. She always allows herself to be led by cultural expectations. I had given up Zahid. I had not fought for him and now I had to live by that decision. I put the phone under my pillow and walked out of the room.

Later that day I spoke to my friend Rabika and confided in her a little about what was going on. I told her that Sarfraz and I were having difficulties and that we couldn't get past them and how I wanted to divorce him. She insisted that things couldn't really be that bad and that I just had to hang on.

"You're lucky. Your man's gorgeous and rich and decent. Plus, you're moved out, living in a gorgeous house. Look at Siedah, she's still living with her hellish mother-in-law. You've got a set-up and a half. What's the problem?"

I wanted to tell her everything - about Yasmin and the constant ache I felt around Sarfraz and how lonely I was and how he used me and left me that night. I wanted to tell her how scared I was that life would always be this empty and that it was killing me inside but instead I simply agreed with her. "You're right, Rabika, you're right. I'm being stupid."

"Hang on to him Kieran. He's a good man."

I agreed and we said our goodbyes and hung up. What was I going to do? I couldn't live like this.

I decided to consult Rayya about a possible divorce. I couldn't just say it to her so I had to think of a way of subtly discussing it. I thought about it for a few days and then suddenly thought of the perfect way to do it. Rayya had once spoken about a friend of hers who wanted a divorce. I could simply start talking about her and so it went…

"How's Nargis?" I said. "Is she still having problems with her husband?"

"Yeah, she's really depressed. She doesn't know what to do," said Rayya.

"Why doesn't she just do it? Get a divorce?"

"It's not that easy, is it? She's got two kids. Who's going to support them? She can hardly go back to her mum's."

"I suppose it would be different if she didn't have kids, right?"

"Yeah, I suppose so."

"But most girls that divorce young usually get married off again, right?"

"You say 'most girls' like it happens often."

"No, I'm just saying. Like if someone my age was to get divorced, her parents would probably try to get her married off again, right?"

"Yeah, most probably. I mean if she didn't have any kids then, yeah, what other option is there? Of course, her parents would more likely kill her before re-marrying even came into the equation."

"Yeah, but it shouldn't be that way. If a girl is really unhappy in her marriage, she should be allowed to end it without worrying about all the stigma that surrounds divorce," I said.

"But as a last resort. If divorce became acceptable in our culture the way it is for white people, can you imagine what would happen? Do you think Mum and Dad would have lasted this long if divorce was common?"

I said nothing.

"Besides, a girl's parents would have a merry old time trying to get her married again, unless it was back home of course. No one wants a tarnished woman."

"True," I said. Those words ran through my mind for days afterwards. *No one wants a tarnished woman.*

Christmas and New Year came and went. I didn't bother hoping that things would get better this year because I knew they wouldn't. Sometimes I wondered if Sarfraz could have done this in a way that I could have accepted. Like, if he had told me his plans before we got married, would I have thought it was a good idea because in theory, it *is* a good idea. Two people who don't want to get married do so but to live as individuals. It's just that I had committed myself to the marriage so wholeheartedly that I fell apart when it all unravelled. Perhaps if he had told me prior to us sleeping together and all the mess that followed, we could have been friends. The prospect of that happening was impossible now. Sometimes I wanted so desperately to contact Zahid but for all I knew, he could be married too now, so I always pushed thoughts of him away. I couldn't allow another person into the equation to confuse things further.

Instead of hoping things would get better, I involved myself at work as much as possible. I worked late since there was nothing else to do with my time, and I became involved with all aspects of the centre. I spent time in the labs learning about the kind of things that went on, I went to the screening clinic, I took an injection to test for H-Pylori and generally became more involved. At home, Sarfraz and I drifted apart more than ever. The last time we had spoken was when he had thrown an unopened envelope from the post into the bin. I had raised an eyebrow at him and he had simply said, "Wrong place, looking for a 'Tyra Zain'." I had simply nodded and gone back to my coffee.

I felt trapped, caged like an animal. It wasn't long before I got bored of work. I was bored of life. Bored of it all. I had had enough of being the archetypal young Asian girl, living a respectable life with a 'respectable' husband. I had started to pray regularly but it didn't give me the peace

I hoped for. I had had enough of it all. I was ready to give up on it all. I had crazy thoughts, the kind that I used to entertain frequently when I was younger. Thoughts of going to sleep and never waking up. Thoughts of just fading away…

It was the 5th of January. The Greenwood New year's party was well under way; raucous laughter floated up to the top deck and ground against my headache. I leaned over the deck of the docked boat and looked over the turbulent Thames. It seemed to be arguing with the dark, angry sky which was threatening to open at any minute. I rubbed my temple and shivered. I had boarded the boat, taken a few random pictures and then walked straight up. I persuaded myself to go and join the party. No doubt I would have to field a multitude of questions about why my husband wasn't here, where my husband was, why he was so busy, etc, but I could handle it, I supposed. I turned to look at my reflection in the dark glass of a cracked window-pane. I wore the same black scoop-neck top I had worn to Ashley's birthday party almost three years ago but this time, I wore it over a black vest so I showed nothing of my chest. *Three years ago,* I thought sadly. I shook my head free of the nostalgia that welled up inside and concentrated on my reflection instead. I brushed my hair and ran my hands over it to calm the static. I righted the wedding ring on my finger which always slid round towards the crook of my finger. I was too small for the ring and didn't quite fill it which, if I was in a particularly philosophical mood, I would have said was a metaphor for my marriage, perhaps for my entire life. I smiled at my inner rambling and exhaled slowly.

I walked downstairs slowly and entered the party by myself. I immediately felt like an alien. People milled around with glasses of red wine engaged in light conversation. My lone figure went unnoticed. I spotted Nicki Sanford, the Lab Manager, and approached her.

"Nicki."

"Kieran!" she exclaimed happily. She was already a little giddy, which was to be expected if the stories of her behaviour at last year's party were anything to go by.

"Hi, Nicki. I left the departmental digital camera with you before. Is it possible I could have it back so I can carry on taking a few pictures for our intranet?" I asked.

"Sure, sweetheart," she replied, slurring her words. She reached into her bag and rummaged through it.

I looked at her expectantly.

"Um… " she looked at me, confused. "It was right here. I know it was right here." She swung the bag onto a ledge and rifled through it again.

Andrew is going to kill me if anything happens to that camera, I thought.

"Ooh! I remember," she said. "I left it in the Ladies. I'll go get it." She started a slow, unsteady walk towards the stairs leading down to the toilets.

"Nicki, I'll get it myself, thanks," I said impatiently as I headed downstairs. I was glad to get away from the noise and the laughter again. It seemed that these days, I couldn't be with people and I couldn't be alone. Familiar feelings took me over as I descended the steps; feelings of hopelessness and helplessness. I was sick and tired of being helpless.

The deafening blast shook the entire boat. Wine glasses crashed to the floor and everyone froze. There was an ominous rumbling and everyone looked to each other for answers. Suddenly, a high whining alarm ripped through the air. Everyone began to move as one.

"Everyone, please, form a single file line!" shouted Linda at the top of her voice. As the Fire Officer, she was trained to handle situations like this but of course, no one listened to her as everyone charged for the exit. Linda had been conscientious enough, however, to grab the list of confirmations against all invitations that had been sent out: in essence, a list that showed who exactly was on the boat and, God forbid, who may still be on there.

People ran off the boat in an increasing panic as the alarm grew louder and more piercing. A sudden explosion from within the boat illuminated the night sky. There were a few screams and a huge amount of confusion as everyone moved away from the burning boat. Multiple people dialled 999 in a panic as a further series of explosions shook the boat.

The fire had grown both in size and ferocity by the time the fire engines came. The heat emanating from it was unbearable. Linda fought her way through the crowd to a fireman who looked like he had some authority.

"I have a list here that should tell us everyone who was on the boat and

I can cross-reference it with who is out here," she said.

"That's excellent. We need to do it as quickly as possible. If we give you a loudspeaker, can you identify the people as fast as possible?" he said.

"Yes," she said, grabbing the loudspeaker. "Can I have your attention please?" she said. "Greenwood staff, can I please have your attention? I have a list of people that were on the boat and who should be here. I will call out your name and please shout if you are here. We need to do this as quickly as possible." Everyone was silent.

"Kieran Ali," she called out. "Kieran Ali! Kieran? Can anyone see Kieran?" Everyone turned to each other in a panic and searched for her.

"Kieran!" shouted a voice. Everyone turned to the voice. It came from Nicki Sanford. "Kieran is downstairs. She went to the toilets to get the digital camera. She was taking some pictures before and she gave it to me and I left it there and… " She trailed off, looking in the direction of the fire. It was quite obvious that the fire had started below deck. One of the firemen was already informing his colleagues.

"Ok, that's one. We need to know how many," said Linda. "Please, you need to concentrate on your name. We need to make this as fast as possible. Jennifer Allen!"

"Here!" yelled Jennifer.

"Karin Ashton!"

"Here!"

"Jonathan Brewster!"

"Here!"

"Gabrielle Crawford!"

"Here!"

And on the list went until they reached the very end without another missing person. Kieran, it seemed, was the only person missing. Linda rushed to the Officer in charge and enquired about the state of the search.

"We can't send any more men on there until we calm down the fire. We will then do a thorough sweep of the boat. I assure you miss, we will do our best, now if you'll excuse me," and with that he walked away.

Like a gift from God, it suddenly began to pour with rain. It went a long way to helping the fire fighters deal with the blaze. By the time they wiped it out, people were in tears from fear, exhaustion and worry. They found no traces of Kieran inside. Linda looked out onto the expansive Thames and scanned the surrounding area. Maybe Kieran had jumped ship and was swimming to safety at this very moment.

After everyone was settled down and a thorough search was made of the boat, Kieran still hadn't materialised. Everyone instantly thought the worst. *Where is she? Is she dead? How did the fire start?* People called her phone to ensure that she hadn't simply changed her mind about the party and headed home but there was only a 'This phone has been switched off' message at the other end.

A cursory inspection of the boat concluded that the fire was exacerbated by Isopropanol, a highly flammable liquid used as a coolant in the engine room. Of course, a more thorough investigation would be carried out to ascertain the exact cause of the fire and what had happened to Kieran but due to the rain and hose water, gathering conclusive evidence of anything seemed doubtful. The firemen urged people to go home but many stayed to find out what was happening. The fire had also attracted a local crowd. After further investigation, the Firemen concluded that the cause of the fire had been an overloaded circuit. There was still no sign of Kieran.

Sarfraz grabbed the phone just in time.

"Mr. Ali?" said an unfamiliar voice.

"Yes?"

"Would you be kind enough to tell me if your wife, Mrs. Kieran Ali, is at home with you?"

"May I ask who is calling?"

"My name is Michael Green. I am the Chief Fire Investigator for the borough of the City of London."

"What's this about?"

"Sir, will you first please tell me if your wife has been in contact with you during the past hour?"

Sarfraz glanced at the time: 8 p.m.

"No, she hasn't. She's at a work thing, a New Year's party. She said she wouldn't get home until a bit later than usual. What's this about?"

"I'm afraid I may have some bad news, sir."

"What bad news?" he asked suspiciously.

"Sir, there has been a fire on the HMS President which was being used to host the Greenwood Institute's New Year's party. She may have been caught in the fire."

"May have? What do you mean? What happened?"

"Well, sir, the fire was caused by an overloaded electrical circuit. Once ignited, the fire fed off a highly flammable chemical called Isopropanol which caused a series of small explosions. It causes intense heat and what with the rain and water we haven't been able to conclude anything more than that."

"Oh my God. How many people are involved?"

"Mrs. Ali is the only person that is missing."

Sarfraz suddenly felt sick. "Only person? What are you talking about? There were meant to be dozens of people at that party. Why is she the only person that is missing?"

"Everyone was upstairs. From our reports, Ms. Ali was at the point of origin at the time of the fire."

"Are you telling me that my wife is dead?" he asked slowly.

"Sir, at this moment that is only a possibility we are investigating."

Sarfraz felt faint. "But surely she wasn't there. I mean, there would be some evidence, wouldn't there?"

"Yes, sir. We have not fully cleared the site. As of yet, we have not found any conclusive evidence. We must also bear in mind that it was on a boat. Mrs. Ali may have tried to escape the fire by swimming away from it."

"But surely if she made it upstairs, she would just use the exit?"

"Logic rarely prevails when a person is in that kind of situation."

"But you're not sure? I mean, she could have just wandered off the boat for a walk or something, right? She could be safe somewhere. You're not sure, right?"

"No sir, we are not sure. That is why we're asking you to ring all her friends and relatives to see if she has been in contact. One of our officers can come and collect you and you can make the calls at our station."

Sarfraz felt numb. What the hell was going on? He said, "Yes," and hung up.

Immediately, he called Kieran's family home and all her sisters' homes to check if she had been in contact. They all said a confused "No". When asked for an explanation, Sarfraz simply said she had mentioned going round to her mum's house after work today and he was wondering if she had gone there. He couldn't think who else to contact. When it boiled down to it, he hardly knew anything about Kieran. They were almost like strangers yet the thought of losing her pulled at his heart. He ran up to her room and rooted through her drawers. Finally, he found a small address book which he put into his pocket. A car came to pick him up and took him to the fire station. There, he made frenzied phone calls to everyone in her phone book asking if she had been in touch. He was angry and confused. In this age of modern technology, they couldn't even ascertain whether she was in the fire or not.

It was almost 4 a.m. before Chief Fire Investigator Michael Green walked into the room. Sarfraz looked up sharply.

"Any news?" he asked shakily. Michael Green walked to Sarfraz's table and sat down resignedly.

"What's happened? Have you found her?" asked Sarfraz.

"Sir, we are still investigating the area but as of yet, there are no signs of Mrs. Ali. We have a member of Greenwood Institute staff who is sure that Kieran was downstairs at the time of the explosion. We have not been able to gather any conclusive evidence either way. The only thing we can assume at this time is that she dived into the Thames and tried to swim away. We have consulted several different sources to see if there were any sightings of her but so far, nothing has turned up."

"She's dead?" finished Sarfraz.

"Nothing is certain at this time but it has been eleven hours since the time of the fire so we are losing optimism." Michael Green lowered his eyes and fell silent.

Sarfraz was numbed by the news. He sat still for a moment and then put his head in his hands and wept like a child. Sobs wracked his body but he didn't care what he looked like. The fire officers left him for a while as he laid his head on the table and sobbed. He couldn't believe it. How could this happen? Kieran? She was a survivor. Yes, she was vulnerable and yes, he had taken a little life out of her but she was a survivor. Something like this was not meant to happen to her. He let tears stream down his face for a few minutes before he tried to gather his thoughts. *What am I going to do? What have I done?* Kieran had been so good to him and he had pushed her away. She had pleaded with him for a bit of warmth. All she wanted was for him to care for her, whether it was as a friend or as a husband but he had spurned every single attempt she had made to make peace between them. And now she was gone. He simply couldn't believe it. He tried to pull himself together. He stood up giddily and went to find Michael Green.

"What happens now?" he asked falteringly.

"You wait. We will do our utmost to find Mrs. Ali whether she is alive or… " he paused. "We will try to find her. Once we've completed our investigation and made official confirmations, you can get in touch with the Births, Deaths and Marriages Office. You will be responsible for sorting out the necessary papers. In the event that we cannot physically confirm Mrs. Ali's death, there is usually a seven year waiting period until they issue you with an official death certificate."

Sarfraz nodded numbly.

"I trust you will contact the rest of her family and her friends?"

Sarfraz nodded again.

"I am very sorry for your loss, Mr. Ali."

"Thank you," replied Sarfraz, choking on the words.

He drove home in a flurry of tears and anger. How could this have happened? It had been his fault. He could have prevented it somehow. She had asked him to attend the party with her and he had refused. If he had gone, things would have turned out differently. He couldn't believe the way he had treated her during the course of their marriage. He had hurt her countless times. He had been sharp and cold to her when all she asked for was a bit of warmth. She was like a little girl. She had this edge, a fighter's edge but Sarfraz knew that deep inside, she was vulnerable. It was what attracted him most to her - the fact that she needed his protection. She had this quality that made him want to love her and hold her and consume her. That's why being around her had always been so dangerous; because he found it hard to control himself. And now she was gone. He had forced her to live a lie and put up with a sham of a marriage. He knew she wanted so much more but he had always said no. She had practically begged him to stop seeing Yasmin and commit to the marriage fully but out of his own selfishness, he had said no.

He got home and sat on the sofa for a long time. He had to think about what he was doing. *You obviously don't care for morality or honesty or common decency! Can't you see how wrong this is?* Her voice resonated in his mind. He felt tears gather in his eyes again and tried to shake them off. He picked up the phone and dialled.

Chapter 11. The Beginning

"Ms Tyra Zain?"
"Yes."
"Air Canada, Gate 7, on your right."

It is kinder to give a person closure than to leave them hanging. If I had just run away like I had originally planned, they would have never stopped searching or wondering. It was a crueller punishment than what they were going through now.

Ever since my conversation with Rayya, I had planned to run away. I could not face it any more. By the grace of God, at the time of the fire, I had already sorted out my deed poll papers, new passport, bank accounts and visa for Canada. When I came upon the fire, I saw a way out, an opportunity, and I had reacted with instinct. I didn't even question how the fire started. There was only one thought going through my head: *Get out of here before someone sees you.* I had left quickly and silently. I was not the best of swimmers and even though there was a strong current, I knew that I could make it from the base of the docked boat to land. I carried out the actions on automatic pilot. I knew that a girl walking down the Embankment in dripping clothes would attract attention so I wrung out my scarf and covered my hair with it like a headscarf. I dried myself off the best I could then simply ran away to the backdrop of wailing sirens. I thought of Julia Roberts in 'Sleeping with the Enemy'. I was hardly in the same situation but I remembered how she left without any plans or money. I was better organised. *I can do this,* I thought as I ran away.

And I had. Here I am. Okay.

As I walk up the winding corridor, I can't believe what I have done. It's crazy and stupid and brave but it's also the best thing I could have done for myself and my family. I hope my 'death' will do something to bring the family a little closer. I hope that it will make my mother realise that her daughters are not expendable, that we are not a commodity to be sold to the highest bidder. I hope it will give Sarfraz an excuse not to marry again and to live his secret life with Yasmin however he pleases.

When I look at it from an objective point of view, I don't really hate the people I thought I hated. My mother and brother I pity more than anything. I know their demons will finally consume them one day. Maybe not today, maybe not tomorrow but one day. And as for Sarfraz, he's not a bad guy. It's never as black and white as in the movies. He used me and made me feel worthless but I still hope the best for him. Deep down, I know he is a good guy and maybe one day he will find the peace that so often evaded him during our marriage.

As for Zahid, I can't really think of him because it is too painful. They say love hurts. They say love is a bitch and they're right. Love claws at your heart and tears you up inside. But you know what else it does? It conquers. Thousands of times I wished I had been brave enough to face my father over Zahid. I wished that I had held out and been strong. Things would have been so much easier than what I went through with Sarfraz.

I entertained thoughts of finding Zahid, of telling him how much I loved him, of asking him to come away with me but sometimes the best thing we can do for the ones we love is to just let them go. I know Zahid still loves me and a part of him always will but he doesn't deserve the life I am going to lead, a quiet life in which all family and friends have to be forgotten. He deserves warmth and light and happiness and a wife he can impress with at weddings. He needs life and right now, I am lifeless.

I know I am starting a new beginning and that I should look forward but as I step onto the plane, I can't help but feel sadness for all that I am leaving behind - my family, my friends, my life. I know that it will kill me on cold winter nights. I know I will miss my friends like crazy, I know that I will never be able to speak to Zahid again. I think about the unnecessary pain I am putting everyone through but then I think of the dark days I have been through and I know that it is worth it. I hope that it will make everyone think a bit more or a bit less; think a bit more about religion and a bit less about culture, more about love and less about lust. I hope eventually they will think more about their lives and less about their loss.

Now, I have to take care of myself. I am not going to talk about how I am in control of my life now. I am not going to throw my hands up in salvation for even though the men in my life helped me get to this point, it is I, and only I, that made the decisions that led me here. I always had control of my life, I just refused to take it.

I remember reading a book once where the author wrote about a conversation she had had with a friend.

"Mother was a tall woman," said the friend.

"You must take after your father, then," remarked the author, since the friend was of average height.

The friend smiled and said, "I did not mean in inches. Mother was shorter than I am. That was just soul talk."

I remember believing that *I* was a 'tall woman' because of everything I had been through but now I realise that I wasn't. I was weak and had given in to the expectations others held of me. I, like every other girl in my situation, had a choice. I simply made the wrong one. I chose the path of the coward. I did not have the courage to grab what I wanted. Instead, I allowed myself to be pressured and controlled and moulded into what other people wanted me to be but now I am leaving them all behind.

I try to swallow the lump in my throat but then allow myself a few tears for I am not only leaving behind everything I know, I am also leaving *myself* behind. I am leaving behind my dark memories, the long days and endless restless nights, the insecurity, the pain and the anger. I am leaving behind Kieran Ali.

Printed in the United Kingdom
by Lightning Source UK Ltd.
126889UK00001B/76-87/A